"Your

Keith brushed his lips along her shoulder, then slid the tiny strap of her sunsuit down to caress her breast with his fingertips.

At his touch, Laura moaned and leaned into his body. She felt the rise and fall of his chest, became aware of his rain-soaked jeans.

"You're all wet," she murmured, her voice low and husky.

Smiling slowly, he backed up a step. She heard the thin rasp of his zipper.

His jeans resisted, clinging to his briefs. Finally he muttered a soft "To hell with it," and before Laura could start breathing again, he was standing naked before her....

Regan Forest lives in the desert near Tucson, so she had no lack of inspiration for *Desert Rain*. This highly charged love story was written during a scorching Arizona summer.

All Regan's books reflect her interesting background and life-style and her unique talent for bringing characters to life. This is her third captivating Temptation—with more to come.

Books by Regan Forest

HARLEQUIN TEMPTATION
80–THE ANSWERING TIDE
95–STAR-CROSSED

HARLEQUIN INTRIGUE
24–ONE STEP AHEAD

These books may be available at your local bookseller.

Don't miss any of our special offers. Write to us at the following address for information on our newest releases.

Harlequin Reader Service
901 Fuhrmann Blvd., P.O. Box 1397, Buffalo, NY 14240
Canadian address: P.O. Box 603,
Fort Erie, Ont. L2A 9Z9

Desert Rain

REGAN FOREST

Harlequin Books

TORONTO • NEW YORK • LONDON
AMSTERDAM • PARIS • SYDNEY • HAMBURG
STOCKHOLM • ATHENS • TOKYO • MILAN

This book is lovingly dedicated to Sereta,
who inspired it, and to Bob,
who I wish was here to share
the fun with us.

Published September 1986

ISBN 0-373-25223-4

1

THE SILENCE OF THE ROOM was too deep, the lights too harsh, the air too cold against her shoulders. The eerie feel of midnight. Laura Caldwell closed her reference book and placed it back on the shelf. She turned and crossed to the newspaper section, thinking how unnaturally cool the university library felt at this time of night. Not the artificial cold produced by air conditioning, but a stiff and clinging kind of cold.

Her eyes scanned the vast, book-lined, nearly deserted room. Two students stood on the far side, talking softly; another one sat in the magazine reference section. A man in his late thirties —an extraordinarily handsome man wearing jeans and a white short-sleeved shirt—was reading at one of the tables. His concentration seemed centered on the book, his head resting on his palms, his fingers lacing through thick dark hair.

He seemed to feel eyes on him, for he looked up and caught her gaze. An instant of communion in a fractured pause of time. A tremor of unease. In those swift seconds Laura knew something was wrong; the man was deeply troubled. Even from across the room she could see the moisture in his eyes. He looked down quickly, self-consciously, and she, out of politeness, turned away.

A stolen glance back saw him slide his fingers despondently through his hair and drop his head onto his arms, as if to shut out everything but his own private thoughts. He knew she had seen his tears, she realized, but his embarrassment had been fleeting, forgotten already under the burden of his heavier thoughts. Her heart went out to the stranger goaded by the prickling of her curiosity, even though he no longer seemed to be aware of her.

Laura spent the next half hour searching through local newspapers for articles on prominent Tucson women with young families. It was late to be researching her talk on "Living with Your Teenager" for a local career women's group, but this had been her first chance today to get to the library.

She had been held up with one of her clients, a sixteen-year-old girl who had been arrested for shoplifting. Even now, concern for the girl crowded her thoughts, a persistent rustling in the back of her mind. This case troubled Laura. The girl was so personable, yet full of remorse and rebellion at the same time, burdened with the weight of secrets.

When Laura came from behind the shelves into the main reference room again, the man was sitting just as he was before, with his head on the table. Probably he had fallen asleep. When the lights blinked overhead to announce the library closing, which meant it was 2:00 A.M., he raised his head slowly and closed his book.

Swinging the strap of her bag over her shoulder, Laura hurried past him toward the exit. Out of politeness, she didn't look in his direction again, but she wanted to . . . and not just because he seemed so troubled. She would have liked to see if he was as handsome on second impression as he was on the first, for no other reason than that she appreciated masculine beauty.

Outside, the night had cooled. There was a freshness left by an afternoon summer rain, the balmy fragrance of desert over the grassy, cultivated landscape of the campus. In the glow of a full moon the shadowy peaks of the Santa Catalina mountains rose against the north sky. Laura walked listlessly under the sprawling eaves of the enormous library building toward a slope of lawn that slanted to the narrow street and the parking lot. Fewer than a half dozen cars remained at this late hour.

She paused for a moment on the brow of the slope before she started down into the night. Perfume from flowering bushes hung in the air. Her filmy pink skirt caught the light as she crossed under the streetlamp; wisps of her blond hair moved about her forehead in a small breeze. High heels hampered her, but she suddenly felt a need to hurry. The deserted campus trembled with foreboding shadows.

She had seen no one, no movement at all. But as she fumbled with her keys to unlock her car, Laura felt a presence behind her only seconds before she was seized roughly around the shoulders. A heavy hand came over her mouth to muffle her cry of alarm. Gripped by terror, Laura struggled to free herself from the hold of a man she couldn't see.

She fought violently, feeling as much as hearing the threats breathed into her ear, aware of the flash of a knife blade in the white light of the moon, experiencing the horror of being overcome by the force of raw strength.

There was a wild gasp and a cry of alarm just before her assailant whirled around in panic toward the tall shadow of a man behind him. As the grip of hands loosened, Laura ducked out of the way. She could barely tell what was happening; she only knew that in seconds her attacker had been disarmed and was scurrying into the bushes.

Breathing hard, she fell back against the side of the car on legs that would no longer hold her. The tall form of a man remained beside her, not touching her. He had started to run toward the criminal, who was already out of sight, hiding somewhere in the shadows. But her rescuer changed his mind about pursuit and turned his attention, instead, to her.

"Are you all right?"

She nodded, breathing in gasps, staring at the knife in the man's hand, which moments before had been held to her throat. "Yes . . . thanks to you . . ." Her voice was weak and shaking.

He set the knife on the hood of the car. "You put up quite a struggle against an armed man."

She didn't answer. Her body sagged and she struggled to keep from losing her balance, and the man reached out to steady her. He caught her full weight as she started to collapse.

Only then, trembling within the shelter of careful, gentle arms, did she sense something strangely familiar. She gazed up at her rescuer in the dusky silver glow of the moon. This was the same man she had seen minutes ago in the library! He stood beside her now, holding her up with one arm while he opened the car door with the other. Then he eased her gently onto the seat.

She drew her hands to her face and trembled. A sob came up from her throat in spite of her efforts to hold it back. "I was . . ." she sputtered. "I was terrified. . . . How can I thank you for what you just did?"

"I didn't do it for thanks." The voice was so soft and so deep that it seemed to be coming from far away.

"You risked your life to confront a man with a knife."

"I didn't risk my life. I've had some experience in. . ." He paused as if he had changed his mind about wanting to explain why it had been so easy for him to disarm a thug. Watching her push her tangled hair away from her eyes, he said, "I think you should just sit there for a few minutes until you stop shaking."

"Will I ever stop shaking?"

"I think so, eventually." He leaned against the top of the car, gazing down at her. "My name's Keith Martin, but I don't expect you to remember that. You've had a hell of a scare."

"I think you just saved my life."

"You shouldn't have been out here alone. They warn women about walking on the campus at night. There have been too many incidents like this one."

"I know..." she answered in the shaking voice. "It was stupid of me, but I...it's hard to have to be...so..." She paused, holding her head in the thin light of the car. "I'm Laura Caldwell. And you're right. I've already forgotten your name."

"It's a forgettable name. Keith is enough. You're in mild shock, Ms Caldwell, and sure in no shape to drive. Do you want a lift someplace? Or do you just want me to stay here with you a while longer?"

"I...don't know. There's no danger now; I wish I could stop shaking."

"I'm shaking myself. Look, if..." He reached for the wallet in his back pocket and whipped out a card. "Here's my faculty identification, just to prove I'm who I say I am—"

She glanced at the card, and interrupted, "You're on the university faculty?"

"Anthropology department."

Nodding numbly, she said, "I've lost...lost my keys. I dropped them when that...man..." Shuddering, she started to rise, but sank back onto the car seat, groaning about knees that had turned to rubber.

He searched the area around the car until he found the keys. "We ought to notify the police."

Feeling the pinch of her teeth against her lower lip, Laura answered, "Do you think so? I'm not hurt and I...I didn't get a look at the man. Oh, I just..." Glancing out at the brooding darkness, she shuddered. "I don't want to have to stay here . . . to wait for the police."

"I don't blame you, but you were assaulted, and *I* got a look at him." He paused thoughtfully, brushing back his hair with his fingers. "If you're up to it, I'll buy you a cup of coffee at Mackey's around the corner. I can phone the police from there, if that's okay with you. And you do look like someone who could use a cup of coffee."

"I guess you're right; this should be reported, especially if you saw the man. What did he look like? No, never mind, I don't want to know . . . I just . . . I don't think I want . . . to be alone right now . . ."

"Why not scoot over? I'll drive across to Mackey's."

Laura hesitated.

"Trust me—it's okay. Although under the circumstances, one can't blame you for being cautious."

"I do trust you, after what you just did for me, but thank you for the reassurance of your ID card, anyhow. It's a bit late for me to get cautious."

"Nah, never too late for that."

She slid over to the passenger side, then he started the engine and drove slowly through the streets of the deserted campus, out onto Speedway Boulevard. Neither spoke until he had pulled into the restaurant parking area.

"I hope I can walk," she said softly.

"Don't worry. I can hold you up."

He circled his arm around her and led her inside the building to one of the booths. The few patrons, all university students, gazed at them curiously, because with her torn dress and her halting steps, Laura appeared to be injured.

While she waited, he ordered coffee. One steaming cup he set in front of her, the other he carried with him to a phone booth just outside the door. Less than five minutes later he returned and sat down across from her.

"The police have dispatched a helicopter to the area to search for a man on foot, but it's no doubt been too long. We should have phoned sooner, I guess. They said since you didn't see your assailant, there's nothing to be gained from talking to you tonight, but to let them know if you think of anything about him that could identify him."

"And you? Do they want to talk to you?"

"Yeah. For a description to make a composite drawing from. They feel this may be the same man who has kidnapped and murdered two other women in the university area in the past eight months."

She stared into the black liquid in her cup. "Keith...I wasn't strong enough to fight him off.... He was determined to force me into my car.... If you hadn't been there..."

"Try not to think about it."

"How can they possibly expect to find him?"

"I was told there's a helicopter in the air at night, within three minutes of anywhere in Tucson. Damn, I wish we'd rushed for the nearest phone in the library, but hindsight's pretty useless."

"I couldn't have rushed anywhere."

"No, you couldn't. I promised to stop by the station and describe the guy for a police artist. It can wait until morning. They have my phone number, meantime, should any suspects turn up, but that's unlikely. The bastard's had more than enough time to disappear."

When Laura lifted the paper cup to her lips, her hand was trembling so violently that she had to put it down again. "I'm sorry I've caused you so much inconvenience."

"I'm not sorry at all. I'm glad I happened to be there."

She sat back and tried to smile. "But it's a ghastly hour. You were no doubt on your way home and I'm keeping you."

"I was at the library because the air conditioning in my apartment isn't working, so the only thing you're keeping me from is the stifling heat."

She had taken several deep breaths, leaning back against the booth, her eyes closed. She opened them now and smiled. "I think I'm starting to relax a bit."

"Good." He sipped his coffee calmly.

She saw again the sadness that had dulled his eyes earlier in the library. It was clouded now but still there—that unmistakable sadness. Grief. She watched him in silence for a time. "You seem so nonchalant about having just fought off a man wielding a knife."

"He didn't put up any fight at all, actually. I was just leaving the library and standing on the slope over the parking lot. I watched you walk under the streetlight. From where I was standing I could see somebody move out of the shadows toward you, and I saw you start to struggle. I haven't run that fast in years. Had to be careful, though; I saw the flash of the knife and I didn't want to get you killed."

"You were so fast. I didn't see how you got the knife from him. Are you used to such encounters?"

"No, but I grew up in a very tough neighborhood. One never forgets the art of self-defense."

His blue eyes studied hers intensely as she picked up her cup again with still-trembling hands and sipped, savoring the welcome taste of hot coffee in a room so frigid with air conditioning that she shivered in her thin dress.

His feet shuffled against the floor. "Do you often stay this late at the library?"

"No. It's just been one of those days when—" Coffee splashed over her hand as she spoke, and she jumped back in alarm. "Oh, look at me shake! I thought I was getting better, but now it's starting again."

"Delayed reaction," he said. "I thought it might happen."

"That man . . ." Laura shuddered. "I can't stop thinking about him . . . about the terror I felt when he grabbed me. I'm glad I didn't see his face. I wouldn't want to have to think about his face. . . ."

Keith's jaw muscles tightened; his teeth clenched. In the bright lights of the restaurant she saw anger flash in his eyes. This man, she thought, would make another man a formidable enemy. He was large and husky; muscles pushed against the shoulders and sleeves of his short-sleeved cotton shirt. The dark, subtle shadows on his face were evidence that it had been many hours, perhaps early morning, since he'd shaved. He looked more like a lumberjack than a university professor.

What would have happened if her assailant hadn't been able to break free of Keith Martin's grip, she wondered. Keith had the knife then; what would he have done to the man who tried to hurt her? She said softly, "I just . . . I need to get home and lie down."

He tilted his head, studying her. "You're not in any shape to drive. Are you?"

"I don't know . . . I . . ."

He drained his cup hurriedly. "You shouldn't try to drive home; you're still in shock. I'm not going to leave you alone at this time of morning after what happened. Tell me where you want to go, and I'll get my car and drive you there. You can pick up your car from the parking lot tomorrow, in daylight."

"Yes . . . I probably am in shock. I admit I'd be very grateful not to have to drive home alone."

He offered his arm again as they were leaving the restaurant, and she accepted it without hesitation.

In silence he drove to the library parking lot and pulled in next to his own car. Being there again bothered Laura more than she thought it would. All her fear came rushing back, and for the first time she felt herself on the verge of tears. With all the willpower she could muster, she suppressed her emotions to spare this man the ordeal of having to deal with a hysterical woman.

He seemed to sense the recurrence of her fear, for his voice and his manner, already gentle, softened even more. He assisted her from her car into his as if she might break. Laura thought of how often she had read in newspapers of attacks such as the one she'd just experienced. She'd wondered how the victims felt, but she hadn't imagined it as it really was—the surge of pure terror, the helplessness and now the growing, almost uncontrollable, anger. What would be happening to her this moment if a stranger hadn't rescued her? It was too terrifying to think about.

Aware of her inward struggle, the anthropologist was talking very little. "Where are we going?" he asked, starting the engine.

"Head north on Swan Road."

"Swan Road . . ." He hesitated. "We'll hit Swan if we go east on Speedway, right?"

She glanced at him sideways. "You're new in Tucson?"

"Yeah, still learning my way around."

"I'll navigate," she said, leaning her head back against the car seat.

He didn't ask any questions of her until they had traveled several miles, and for his deliberate avoidance of conversation, for his understanding, Laura was grateful. She felt she wasn't entirely coherent.

They left the northern confines of the city, the lights around them thinning. Ahead were a few illuminated houses, but very few at this hour of the morning. Beyond was a flat black wall of darkness.

"We're running into a mountain, Laura. Are you still awake over there?"

She raised her head slowly and gazed out the window. "Turn left at the next street. Go slow—the signs are hard to see."

A few minutes later he pulled into a circular drive. There was a porch light on, but otherwise the house looked dark. He could barely see the structure at all, only an entrance formed by a small lighted garden.

"Is anyone here?"

"No. I live alone."

"Are you okay? Do you want me to go inside with you?"

The overhead car light revealed the gratitude in her eyes when she opened the door and looked over at him. "No, really. It's very late. I'll be fine now. I appreciate your help more than I can tell you."

"Try to get some sleep," he said.

Keith didn't pull out of the driveway until Laura was within the sanctuary of her house. Aware of his protective gesture, she turned around in the open doorway to wave goodbye.

Thank heaven for this man, whoever he was. But the closing of the door closed him off from her life. She felt a pang of regret, even a twinge of fear. He was gone and she was alone with the reverberations of her own terror of the hour just past. The familiar comfort of her house wrapped around her gently, though, pulling her back into her own world. Fatigue was settling over her now that the awful tension had passed, and Laura found herself almost too exhausted to think.

Leaving the lights on behind her, she made her way through the house, checking that all the doors and windows were locked. The fear would eventually wear off, she told herself, but tonight she felt frighteningly vulnerable.

Undressing hurriedly, she took only a few seconds to examine the tear in her sleeve before throwing the dress onto the floor in a heap. Minutes later she was in bed with the blanket drawn up to her chin.

She gradually began to warm, and with the warmth came thoughts of the man who had rescued her. His clear, deep voice echoed through her whirling mind. With a shaky sigh, she closed her eyes to retrieve the image of him. A large man with rugged good looks. An anthropologist, he'd said. She could picture him tromping through the nether regions of the earth in search of remote, mysterious civilizations. Imagining him in a classroom was not as easy. But here, in the shadows of a darkened room, she could still feel his gentle touch. Within the peace and security of her bedroom, Keith Martin remained part of the night; he would not leave her thoughts. Just as he had rescued her from the terror of abduction, thoughts of him now rescued her from the horror-filled reflections on what that abduction might have meant. It was as if, in her state of exhaustion and aftershock, Keith was still there, comforting, taking charge.

Her mind filled with images of him. The sadness she had seen in his eyes for those fleeting seconds in the library told her there was turbulence in his life. Turbulence enough to mist his eyes with tears. Yet his burdens, whatever they were, had been put aside during the time he had spent with her. He'd said nothing about himself; his concern had been only for her.

The lonely, distant wail of a coyote drifted over the desert hills. Thoughts of a caring and gentle stranger stayed with her, calming her, as Laura drifted into the down of sleep.

THE SOUND OF BANGING roused her, and Laura came slowly to consciousness. She opened her eyes to a room blanched with morning light that shone through closed white curtains. The knocking was not the usual morning greeting of the cactus woodpecker hammering on her roof. Fighting the tug of sleep, she listened. Someone was knocking on the window behind the drapes and calling to her. The sound of her own name, muted through glass, brought her all the way up to wakefulness. It was Bernie.

"Laura, can you hear me? What's going on in there?"

"I just woke up!" she yelled. "Hang on a minute!"

Pulling herself stiffly to a sitting position, Laura realized she was sore all over. Stretching painfully, she noticed bruises on her arms. Her left leg throbbed. So distraught had she been over the frenzied struggle last night that she hadn't realized then she had been hurt. When the covers were pushed aside, she found the bruise on her leg—probably the result of a kick of a man's shoe. Wincing, she tried to persuade herself that last night was past, and this morning was like any other. But it was not like any other, even though the dove calls from the garden were the same and the shadows of the giant saguaro cactus trees against the morning sun were the same, and the summer sun sparkled against her mirror the way it always had.

She blinked at the clock. After eight! No wonder Bernie was banging on her window with concern. She had arranged to be there at seven o'clock to help Laura paint the porch before the morning got too hot. It had been years since Laura had slept past 6:00 A.M..

She padded groggily through the house and through the kitchen in her short nightie to let Bernice in the back door.

"What's going on?" her friend repeated, shaking short red curls as she bounded into the kitchen. "Are you all right?"

"Yeah. I just had a very late night."

Bernice, dressed in jeans and a paint-spattered T-shirt, drew back in alarm at the sight of her friend. "Laura, your arms are bruised. And your leg! What happened to you?"

Laura sighed, not wanting to relive the experience of last night, even in her thoughts.

"Laura?" Bernice stared at her eyes. "Where were you last night?"

"At the university library."

"What?" Bernice raised both freckled arms in an exaggerated gesture of frustration. "The library? You spent an evening at the library and came home looking like this?"

Laura grinned. She spooned coffee into the coffee maker, giving all her attention to that small job and not looking at her best friend. A lock of hair fell into her eyes; she pushed it back with her arm. "It turned out to be one of the most exciting nights of my life."

"Don't do this to me, Laura. You know how I hate suspense." Bernie's husky voice dropped almost to a whisper. "What happened to you?"

Laura closed her eyes. It hadn't been a dream; it had really happened. The bruises were real, the night was real and a man named Keith Martin, with the most intriguing face she'd ever seen, was real.

She turned to look at her friend. "Bernie, give me ten minutes to jump in and out of the shower and get dressed. By that time the coffee will be ready. Then I'll tell you."

Bernice stared. "Why am I getting the feeling that we aren't going to be painting your porch, after all, this morning?" Scowling, she sat down and unfolded the morning paper she had brought in from the driveway, muttering something Laura couldn't quite hear about getting bruises in a library.

Laura reflected, while washing her hair in the shower, that sleeping late was such a regrettable waste of time. By getting up so late she'd lost the best part of the day on her morning off, and Bernie was right; the porch wasn't going to get done. Laura felt strange and stiff and sore, and not at all in the mood to immerse herself in the job of painting.

Two bright yellow mugs were already poured full of coffee by the time Laura returned to her sunny kitchen dressed in jeans and an oversize shirt that almost drowned her small frame in folds of white cotton. Bernice set the newspaper aside at once and waited, tapping her nails impatiently while Laura took a slow, grateful sip of the coffee.

"I hope you're not going to tell me you fell down the library steps!"

"What I did was even dumber than that, Bernie. I walked back to my car alone at two in the morning."

The other woman paled. "Oh, no! Laura! After the warnings of so much crime lately in that area? Oh—" Her voice broke. "I'm afraid to hear what you're going to tell me."

"Well, obviously I'm alive to say it, and perfectly fine except for these bruises. But it could have been a very different story. A man with a knife jumped out of the shadows and grabbed me and tried to force me into my car. I struggled with him, but I wasn't aware I was hurt till this morning. I must have been in shock last night."

The hot coffee felt good inside her stomach. Never had Laura appreciated the taste of fresh-brewed coffee as much as she did this morning; never had she found so much joy in the songs of the birds, or the dance of sunlight on the leaves outside, or the companionship of a good friend who cared. Never had she appreciated so much just being alive.

Bernice reached across the table and touched her arm. "Laura, will you *please* go on? How did you get away from him?"

"I never could have, alone. He was disarmed and scared off by a guy who happened to be coming from the library and saw the whole thing."

Bernice's green eyes grew wide. She was silently mouthing the word *disarmed*. "You were *rescued*? By a stranger? Who? Who was he?"

"He's on the faculty, in the anthropology department, and new in Tucson. I didn't even ask where he was from. I didn't ask him anything, I was so traumatized. Now, in the light of morning, I wish I knew more about him."

"It's incredible! A real live Lone Ranger! Did you at least get his name?"

"Sure, a name. Keith Martin. He was wonderful, Bernie. He bought me coffee afterward, and when he saw how shaken I was, he insisted on driving me home."

"Yeah? His car or yours?"

"His. I'd be in your debt if you could drive me down later so I can retrieve mine. Didn't you notice my carport was empty?"

"No, I didn't come around that side of the house; I came through the garden gate." Bernice took her first swallow of coffee since they had begun to talk. "You had a close call, Laura, do you know that?"

"I do know. The police think the man may have already killed two women in the area of the campus."

"The murders we've read about? Oh, my God! Laura! How are you holding up so well? I think I'd be a nervous wreck if the same thing happened to me."

"I was a zombie last night, but today it seems almost like a dream."

"Did you see his face? The guy who grabbed you?"

"No, but Keith did."

"He did? Then they ought to be able to find him. They'll know who to look for."

Laura rubbed her forehead, her eyes closed. "Yes, they have a good chance now. It's likely Keith has saved more lives than just mine."

Bernice touched her friend's hand gently. "I don't think you should go to work today."

"Working is the best thing I could do, I'm sure. If I just carry on as though nothing had happened, I'll forget faster. Besides, I have to put my notes together for my women's group speech tonight. I can't cancel the speech."

"Can't you just do the speech, then, and cancel your clients? How can you concentrate on someone's mental health when you've had such a close brush with . . . Lord knows what?"

"You know I've learned to separate my own problems from those of my clients. I had to or I could never have kept working after Matthew was killed."

"You couldn't work for a couple of months after you lost Matthew."

"This is minuscule in comparison."

"True, but I still feel you aren't objective enough about your cases. You get very involved, especially since you've been working with juvenile court."

"These are kids in need, Bernie. They're at a crossroads where their future can go either way, depending on choices they make now. I'll admit I get involved, but I can't help it. Sometimes I'm the only adult they can talk to."

Bernice shrugged. "Which means you're going to work today whether I advise it or not. So. Tell me about this mystery man who is anthropologist by day and rescuer of ladies in distress by night."

"I told you I know almost nothing about him, except that he's the best-looking guy I've seen in years."

A spark of excitement flickered in Bernice's eyes. "Are you serious?"

"Dead serious."

"I'm stunned! I detect a note of real interest! *You* showing interest in a man after all these years?" Bernice slapped the table in her excitement. "This is really something!"

"Maybe it's just gratitude," Laura said with a smile.

Her friend and fellow therapist frowned, pulled back a little and answered softly, "Hell, maybe it is."

"Don't say that. I don't want to hear that. I noticed this man earlier, in the library. A woman would have to be unconscious not to notice him."

"Hmm, I'll be damned. I hear the woman talking, not the learned scholar. This is a switch. Enthusiasm over a man! Is he single?"

"I assume so. No typical married man would be hanging around the library all night alone because the air conditioning is broken in his apartment."

Bernice looked skeptical. "With men, who can be sure of anything?"

Laura remembered that Keith Martin had been very troubled last night. "You're right, who can?" She rose to refill her coffee mug, standing for a moment in front of the window to gaze out at her back garden. Roses were blooming and doves were calling in a morning filled with the peace of late desert summer.

The world looked so different today. Was it because she'd escaped with her life last night? Or was it because of the man who'd rescued her? Even the Ph.D. she had worked so hard for couldn't help her understand why the world looked so strangely fresh.

It must have been much too long since she'd taken real notice of the beauty around her. Six years since Matthew had crashed one stormy night in his private plane. Six years of adjustment, and of devotion to her career as a clinical psychologist in private practice. Before Matthew, there had been school and working to finance her studies.

In her last year of graduate school she had met Matthew and married him soon after. Their three-year marriage had been happy. It was Laura's choice that not one of the many male friends who filled her life since Matthew's death had ever become a lover.

Bernice, feet propped on another chair, was reading her mind. "Are you going to see the Lone Ranger again?"

"I don't know. If I had the nerve, I'd call him and thank him again for what he did."

"You should! Didn't you say your assailant was armed with a knife?"

"A huge knife. Keith took it away from him."

"So he risked his life to save you."

"He actually did," she agreed, thinking back to last night. Yet he had been so calm, barely winded, as if he did that sort of thing all the time. She turned from the window and sat down again across from Bernice at the small table.

"So are you going to find him and thank him?"

"I want to, but I don't know what to say."

Bernice grinned. "Maybe he'll call you."

"I doubt it. My number's not listed and I didn't give it to him."

"Then it's your move, isn't it?"

A fleeting fear grazed Laura's eyes before she smiled with renewed confidence. In the lens of her mind she had seen an image of Keith's face again, and the image stirred her in unfamiliar, intriguing ways. A flutter of excitement weaved through her, excitement mixed with trepidation.

"I'm all confused," she said softly into her coffee cup. "I have to think about this. Everything feels so strange this morning. I need a little time to think."

2

HIS OFFICE at the university was small and crowded with overstuffed bookshelves and papers stacked high on the desk. Here he spent quiet hours between his classes working on a book manuscript and evading the shadows that hung over his private world.

On the afternoon Laura came, three days after her scare in the library parking lot, he was reviewing an osteology paper with a graduate student. He looked up to see her standing in the doorway, simply waiting, listening to the conclusion of his conversation. Wearing a cotton dress of mint green and pale pink and high-heeled sandals, she looked cool and pastel soft. For a moment, caught by surprise, he stared, drawing into his consciousness the spirit of her beauty. Short blond hair worn full around her face in wispy curls, small, even features, shiny pale pink lipstick, pearls at her ears. She stepped inside the room, smiling, as the student took his exit.

"Dr. Martin, I found you easily in the faculty directory, and since I was just passing by. . ."

Keith rose from his chair. "This is an unexpected pleasure."

"I apologize for eavesdropping on your consultation just now. Osteologic criteria for ethnic differentiation? You anthropologists see everything in the world in comparison to something else."

He smiled. "Everything in the world is relative to everything else. There's no other way to see it."

"Really? Maybe you could..." Laura hesitated when she became aware of what she was about to say, for fear of what he might think. Then, because he seemed so genuinely glad to see her, she decided to say it, anyway. "Might you explain that to me sometime?"

"Sure. I'll mark it on my calendar under 'things I'm looking forward to.'"

His response, delivered with a smile, pleased Laura and put her at ease. She circled the small room slowly, stopping to read the titles under two framed black-and-white photographs. "Thomas Henry Huxley. Franz Boas. I've heard of T.H., but would you introduce me to Franz?"

"Franz is the founder of the American school of anthropology."

"Oh!" She brightened. "Dr. Martin, you should have your portrait done now, while you're in your prime. Think how outstanding you'll look in hallowed halls in contrast to these scowling old men. Why do great scholars always scowl?"

"Maybe they take life seriously. Life's too important to be taken seriously." He sat on the edge of his desk, rubbing his chin, admiring the grace with which she moved. "What makes you think I'd ever become a portrait in a hallowed hall?"

"Because any man with this many books and papers piled on his desk has to be a great scholar. So please don't wait to be photographed until you, too, are stern and scowly and wearing a stiff black suit."

Keith laughed. "An anthropologist with grit would prefer to die young from the poisoned arrows of headhunters than to grow stern and scowly in old dark halls."

"I see. You're a *field* kind of scholar. Well, that seems all the more reason I shouldn't waste what little time you have left. I'm probably keeping you from something important, and I haven't told you why I came. I wanted to thank you again for risking your life for me, and probably saving mine."

He motioned her to a chair, but she seemed either too hurried or too nervous to want to sit down. "I worried about you and wanted to make sure you were all right, but I didn't know how to get in touch with you."

"I'm all right. Thanks to you."

More relaxed now, he smiled. "Good. You look all right. In fact, you look terrific."

She smiled. "The police came to my house the next morning and asked a few questions, but I wasn't much help. Have you heard anything?"

"About the arrest of a suspect, you mean? No, nothing. The guy was young, Laura. I think he may even be a student, and probably smart enough to lie low for a while. But eventually they'll find him. With the drawing, it's just a matter of time."

He studied her face; her eyes skittered away from him to scan the pictures and diplomas on the wall. It was impossible to tell what she was thinking, but she had taken the trouble to come to his office to thank him in person. He was becoming aware that he didn't want her to walk out again as suddenly as she had come in. "Laura," he said briskly, "how about having dinner with me one evening soon?"

She hesitated. Her smile came slowly, stiff at first, then unflexed to ease, then warmth. "I'd like very much to have dinner with you, Keith, but I'm the one who owes you the dinner."

"I'm old-fashioned. I wouldn't feel comfortable with that."

She thought a moment, both hands thrust deep into the pockets of her skirt. "In that case, the solution is for you to allow me to make dinner for you. I'm not a wonderful cook or anything, but I do have my enchilada specialty."

"I have a weakness for enchiladas."

"Good. Then you'll come. What about tonight?"

He looked away swiftly, realizing she had seen uncertainty in his eyes. "Uh . . . tomorrow would be better for me than tonight."

"Okay. Tomorrow, then. You're sure?"

He smiled. "Laura, nothing would give me greater pleasure than to have dinner with you tomorrow night."

"Around seven?"

"Great. All I need are some directions through those roads in the foothills. There are so many turns and winding streets—it's like a maze up there."

THE PROSPECT of seeing Laura Caldwell again brightened an otherwise dismal day for Keith. At breakfast his daughter had been sullen, complaining again, blaming her problems with school and the juvenile authorities on their move to Tucson. There was no question that her defiance over the move had made things worse, and for this Keith blamed himself. Perhaps it had been a mistake to come, but his daughter had been on a collision course with trouble for two years now; uprooting her had been the only means he knew of trying to get her headed down a different path.

Tomorrow was Friday. Tina had already asked permission to spend the night again with her friend, whose mother seemed eager to have her. It had been Mrs. Cotter's idea for Tina to stay over the night the air conditioning went out in the Martins' apartment. Kim was new at school, too, and the girls had met the first morning at the bus stop. They were already fast friends, which was good, but the hollow feeling nagged Keith that his daughter seemed to want to be away from home whenever she could. Still, her being at Kim's would allow him to accept Laura's dinner invitation without guilt.

He knew any escape from guilt was only fleeting; it was something Keith had lived with for more years than he wanted to remember. Deep, unresolved guilt for the circumstances of his daughter's illegitimate birth. Guilt for not knowing how to be a father, for not always being there for her. Guilt for what he'd put Tina, and himself, through during his short marriage because he'd wanted his daughter to have a caring stepmother. Nancy had been anything but caring, and the strained relationships that had resulted from his mockery of a marriage seemed to have triggered Tina's rebellion.

Since his divorce from Nancy, the girl had come away from a half dozen school psychologists well aware of her father's failures. He should have told his daughter, the counselors all said, that her parents had never married. He shouldn't have told the lie about her mother being dead. Hell. What did those psychologists know about the pain of having to tell a child her mother wanted to give her up for adoption? What right did they have to tell him what he should or shouldn't have done?

He had barely known her mother; he'd dated her only two months before she'd become pregnant. Though she had resolved to give up the child, he had preferred marriage to that option, even a loveless one. But the girl's wealthy family had refused. Keith, knowing firsthand what it was to be an abandoned child, was desperate. Unable to bear not knowing the baby's fate, he had sought legal help and learned of his right to block the giving up of the child for adoption. He had fought for and was granted full custody of his illegitimate daughter himself.

He was so young then—only twenty-two—and it hadn't been easy. But dwelling on failures didn't help. He'd hoped this move to another city, a new environment, would offer them both a fresh start. If anything, it had made things worse. Tina had never been in trouble with the law before.

She insisted she had shoplifted the cosmetics only on a dare, but Keith knew the matter went much deeper, back to her resentment of him. That resentment had been fueled by her school psychologists. They had convinced her that her father had never given her a proper home life, and therefore it was he, not Tina, who was to blame for all their problems. Tina was good at doling out that blame. After all, she'd been well taught. Now she was seeing a court-appointed psychologist and it was out of Keith's hands to stop it. He was certain this counseling, more than anything else, would cause what little communication he and Tina had left to break down.

Through the emotional bleakness of the past several days, thoughts of Laura came like a fresh summer wind. And his thoughts kept floating back to her all afternoon, at unexpected times in the classroom during discussions of Australopithecus fossils. He looked forward to seeing Laura again more than he had looked forward to anything for a very long time.

THE DESERT skirting the uphill streets of the Santa Catalina foothills was brushed with the paling light of early evening. The higher north he drove, the larger and farther scattered were the estates, until ahead was the black ledge of mountains that formed a barrier to the crawling fingers of civilization.

Laura's house was just short of this blue-gray line where the foothills turned sharply skyward into stern, rock-carved mountains. The earth-colored stucco nestled into the shadows of the saguaro forest as if it were one with the desert. From the entrance there was no hint of the gracious house within, or of the luxurious poolside gardens behind it.

In a landscape of dense desert, the house faced south toward the valley lights. He parked and entered through the ornate iron gate to a tiny garden of ferns, flowers and a small, splashing fountain, and at the end of its short stone path, the hand-carved door to the private world of a woman he had yet to know.

In the muted light of the doorway she greeted him wearing lavender silk, a flowing blouse, matching straight skirt slit to above the knee, dangling silver earrings and silver sandals—not the same woman he'd met in the shadows of terror down below, in the city. But there had been hints of this woman yesterday—a self-confident, glamorous, extremely intelligent woman.

She led him through a sun-roofed foyer to a living room. With its view of the scalloped circle of mountain ranges and the sprawling city stretched between. it seemed to open out to the world.

Laura in pale lavender and the softness of her mischievous blue eyes and the musical ring of her voice captivated him in a new way, as if he were seeing her now for the first time.

"You look wonderful," she said. "You're smiling and there are no wrinkles in your forehead."

"Did you expect wrinkles in my forehead?"

"You had wrinkles the other night, in the library, and even a little one or two in your office yesterday."

He nodded slowly. "And you, m'lady, are very different from the woman I met Monday night."

"The woman you met then was too traumatized to be herself. I was traumatized for two days."

"That's understandable."

She motioned him to a white velvet sofa. "Please sit down. Will you have a marguarita?"

"Sure, if you'll join me."

"They're already prepared in the blender. I'll only be a second."

The restfulness of the house was what he noticed most. Its colors of earth, its blending with the desert landscape, its wide, uncurtained windows welcoming the wind and sky. The peaceful house, in its compatibility with nature, spoke much about its mistress.

She handed him a long-stemmed glass and sat on the matching sofa across a dark, carved table, facing him. "I'm pleased you could come. A dinner is a pretty understated way of thanking a man for saving your life."

"I'm glad for the chance to get to know you."

"Yes, I am, too."

He smiled a slow, crooked smile. "I'm impressed as hell with this house. It has a real feel of desert."

"Do you like the desert?"

"I'm not sure yet. I'm in awe of it, fascinated by it. There's a hostility about the desert, but I can see you live in harmony with it."

"I do. But only by letting the desert around me remain itself. It stubbornly resists change." She sipped her drink and studied him in silence for a time. "When I saw you in the library Monday night, I couldn't help but notice that you were terribly upset about something."

He shifted with discomfort. "I felt lousy that night, but I hoped it wasn't as obvious as that."

"I'm afraid it was. You looked like a man who had just lost his best friend."

"I had . . . lost a good friend . . ."

She waited through a tense silence.

"A friend died?"

"Yeah . . ." He had no sooner offered this admission than he regretted it because it begged more questions from her. He wasn't about to admit to this sophisticated woman that he was past the point of tears because his personal life was out of control, that his daughter had been arrested, that the little dog he'd loved had died. . . .

"I'm sorry," she said gently. "I was quite concerned about you . . . when I saw you that night."

He squirmed and sought to turn the conversation in another direction, not wanting to think of his pet's death now, or to remember the piercing pain of Tina's rebellion. "It had been a rough day made worse by the heat and my broken air conditioner and my daughter's unhappiness about our move to Tucson."

Laura's eyebrows rose. "You have a daughter?"

"Tina's in high school. You may know how kids feel about having to move to a new city and leave their friends."

"Yes, I do know." She looked at him sideways. "You haven't a wife, too, have you?"

"I'm divorced."

"Recently?"

"More than two years ago."

"And your daughter lives with you?"

"Yes," he answered softly. He didn't know her well enough to explain that his daughter was not the product of his short marriage. It was so much simpler to let people assume his ex-wife was his daughter's mother. The past was very private to him; it was his and Tina's alone, and certainly had nothing to do with this world into which they were seeking a new start.

Keith paused for another drink from the salt-rimmed glass, then sat back and studied her face, holding her gaze. "What about you, Laura? You've told me nothing about you."

"There isn't much to tell about me. I've been a widow for the past six years. My husband died in a plane crash. He was an architect, fairly well-known in southern Arizona. This house is one of his designs."

"No children?"

"Regrettably, no. I like kids a lot—in fact, I work primarily with children."

"Are you a teacher?"

"No, a psychologist."

He winced, feeling as if he'd just been stabbed with something sharp. A sinking stomach came from a sense of loss—sudden loss of respect for a woman to whom he was so attracted. He had to look away, but he knew she was keen enough to observe a negative reaction, however hard he tried to conceal it.

"Wow!" Laura breathed softly, sitting back as if to distance herself from her guest. "I hit a nerve! What do you have against psychologists that can cause the very color of your eyes to change? They went from blue to gray in one cold flash!"

He blinked, not wanting to hurt her. It seemed important not to hurt her. "I just...wouldn't have guessed, that's all.... You're not a school counselor, are you?" He hoped he was able to disguise the dread behind his question.

"No, I'm in private practice. But I often work with kids referred to me by the juvenile court. It's become rather a . . . specialty." She was observing him very carefully; it was obvious he wasn't a bit happy with this answer. There was something like shock in his eyes; he knew it and couldn't stop it.

"Keith, why are you looking at me so strangely?"

"I'm sorry. I didn't mean to look at you strangely."

"One doesn't have to be very astute to see you don't think much of psychologists. I'd appreciate it if you'd open up and tell me why."

Keith sighed deeply, regaining the composure he had lost through the unexpected shock. Shadows of evening had begun to darken the room. Shades of pink and orange streaked the sky in the west and tinted the white walls of the room. An orange glow shone on Laura's fair hair and on her flawless skin. Sophistication, he realized, was so much a part of her that she wore it like a well-fitting gown.

What she was asking of him was an honest answer to a very direct question. He could take a coward's way out and not answer, but if he did he would be closing a door on what friendship they might develop. Had she been any other woman, telling him she was a psychologist specializing in kids with problems, he would have slammed shut the door quickly and solidly. But she wasn't any other woman. And faced with an ultimatum, he knew he didn't want to close any doors . . . at least not now, not yet.

The alternative was to answer her question with enough honesty to satisfy her. But no way in hell would he tell her about his problems with his daughter. She'd see his failures as a parent, and he couldn't stand the thought of being judged by her. The fact that she said she worked with the juvenile court made it even worse.

An awkward silence ensued while Laura waited for an answer. "I've . . . known several psychologists in my lifetime," he began carefully. "When I was a kid I was constantly being dragged to one counselor after another. I was a . . . discipline problem, and these probing strangers were always trying to straighten me out."

Laura didn't speak until she was certain he wasn't going to go on without some urging. "I take it they didn't straighten you out?"

"No. They always asked the same damn questions about my life, my private thoughts. I got sick to death of talking. Pretty soon I just made things up. They were . . ." He paused, thinking he shouldn't say it.

"Gullible?"

He glanced up in surprise. "Yes. Exactly."

She nodded. "Are you talking about school counselors?"

"Mostly. I admit I was a brat. I kept them snowed and they kept me out of school sports, saying I was too aggressive and might hurt someone. Punishment because I wouldn't cooperate."

Laura fell into silence for a time. As Keith waited for her to start the familiar barrage of questions, he stiffened with the old, familiar dread, waiting.

"Well, I can understand," she said finally. "If you had bad experiences with counselors as a kid, you probably carry a hefty resentment. I probably would, too, if I'd been in your place. I hope counseling has improved since you were young, Keith." She paused, then continued hesitantly, "I hope some us are wiser. And I hope like the devil we never do more harm than good, as your counselors obviously did."

This was the last thing he expected her to say. He sat back and took a long drink from his glass. Finally he chuckled. "I thought you'd start asking me questions."

"About what?"

"About why I was such a rotten kid."

She smiled broadly. "I was a rotten kid myself."

"Yeah? Did you hate your counselors?"

"I never had a counselor, but I could have used a good one. I think that's why I wanted to get into this work. My own childhood was less than happy. My father was a tyrant and all I wanted was to get away from home."

He tried to picture her as a little girl, small and delicate and helpless, and unhappy. Scowling, he muttered, "I guess when kids have problems, it usually goes back to their—" Abruptly he cut himself off. What he knew intellectually and what he could deal with emotionally were not balanced for him and never had been. What he knew was painful.

"Usually, yes, it's the home life."

His eyes met hers. "You're not going to do it, are you, Laura? You're not going to analyze me."

She laughed, but she could feel he was extremely sensitive to the subject. "You mean because I'm a psychologist and you were once a rotten kid?"

He laughed then, too, and felt a burden start to ease within him. The directness of her approach left him with no escape, or even the need for one. "Madam, I apologize for thinking bad things."

"Let's drink to that, then," she said, raising her glass. "Oh, your glass is empty. There's plenty more. Let me refill it."

He watched the sheen of lavender shimmer in light when she rose, and he caught the subtle scent of her perfume when she passed near him. Welcoming evening's sanctuary from the day's sapping heat, Keith drew on Laura's presence and her refreshing cool. The obligatory discussion, which she had initiated, would stay behind with the day. He reflected on the caverns of mystery behind the walls of Laura Caldwell's private world.

When she returned and handed him a fresh margarita, he smiled into her blue eyes, past the veils of mystery surrounding her. "I'm glad our chance meeting has resulted in this evening, Laura. One has to wonder about chance sometimes, if there really is such a thing, or if it's destiny."

Her gaze lingered on his face. "Destiny, perhaps. I can't forget that you risked your life for mine."

3

FROM HER GLASS-WALLED DINING ROOM they could see the city lights shimmering through the valley like a spill of diamonds. After dinner they sat with soft music in the background, the sky darkening, the candle flames brightening. They were sipping chilled Chablis and watching the last fading rays of a magnificent sunset.

It was Keith who finally broke their companionable silence. "Can a man overdose on beauty? The sunset, the city lights, the woman across from me? I hope this isn't just a fleeting moment."

"It doesn't have to be fleeting, does it?"

In response, Keith moved his fingers over hers. His touch was so gentle that she barely felt it physically, only emotionally.

"I don't know when I've enjoyed an evening so much. Fantastic company. Great meal . . ."

"You flatter me, Keith. Cooking isn't one of my major interests."

"What are your major interests?"

"My work is, and my house. I love decorating and gardening and tennis and hiking and romantic novels."

"You're a romantic?"

She felt the gentle pressure of his hand on hers. "I haven't thought of myself as such, but there must be something of the romantic in me. It's been hidden for quite a while."

"Why?"

"I don't know why. I . . . guess I've allowed myself to get too wrapped up in my work."

"You really enjoy your work?"

"Yes, very much. Do you?"

"Yeah, though I prefer research to teaching."

"What branch of anthropology are you in? Cultural? The Indians? Lost tribes of headhunters?"

"No, physical. Human origins."

"Ah. Then the field research you talked about must be digging for fossils on the Dark Continent. Have you done that?"

"Sure have. But most of my research has been in a lab."

"I'd like to hear about your work."

He smiled softly. "And I'd like to tell you about it sometime, but this isn't the right atmosphere for dwelling on brittle old fossils."

The still air held the song of the desert: the lonely call of an owl, night insects chirping around them. "We . . . could go out on the deck if you like," she said. "It's lovely once the sun has gone down."

He rose. "Lead, and I will follow."

They stood in shadows, looking out over the lights of the valley. He slipped his arm lightly around her waist.

"Tell me about you," Laura coaxed. "I know only that you're teaching physical anthropology and you have a daughter and you were once a rotten kid who intensely resented his school psychologists. I hope your resentment of the psychology profession won't carry over to me."

"Why would it?"

"It easily could. I saw the resentment at once."

"You're nothing like them. They always wore weird shoes. Why was that, do you suppose?"

"I don't know," she replied, smiling.

"Not silver sandals, not ever."

"Of course not. Not while trying to put you in touch with your hostility. Right?"

"Right on the nose. I finally figured out they meant that I needed to find something or someone to blame for my own aggressive behavior."

"Your parents?"

"I didn't have parents. Just a series of foster homes. I was moved around a lot because I was incorrigible." It pleased him to be able to talk so easily to her about a part of his life he rarely spoke of to anyone.

"No wonder you were bitter," she commented softly. "Are you still?"

"I don't think so."

"You've had a good many slings and arrows in your life."

He grinned. "There were plenty. At least till I was fourteen. That summer I hired out to do yard work for a lady in her sixties. She took special notice of me because I researched the types of trees she had before I trimmed them so I'd do it right. This little thing impressed her and started a friendship, which resulted in her adopting me. Doris was a wealthy widow who'd lost her only son when he was about my age. She was wonderful; she became the mother I never had. Shared my fascination for anthropology and put me through college. I swear, Laura, no human being ever did more for another than my adopted mother did for me."

Her eyes misted as he spoke so casually of a childhood spun of loneliness and pain, and of his love for the mother who had come to him so late. . . .

He cleared the huskiness from his voice. "So there's my dull story, Madam Doctor. Would it be Dr. Caldwell, by some chance?"

"It would."

"As I suspected. Why didn't you say so?"

"You didn't say so when you introduced yourself, did you? What should I have said? I'm Laura Caldwell, Ph.D." She chuckled. "My father says it stands for piled high and deep. He isn't too impressed with my accomplishments."

"I'm impressed." His arm around her waist gently increased its pressure.

A distant coyote's wail filled the deep silence of the desert. A gentle breeze floated over them. Calm. And within that calm, Laura was astounded by her reaction to the touch of this man. It was strangely natural after such a long time. Forgotten sensations returned at this man's touch. Stirrings so long motionless, suspended in air like an abandoned web, gathering only dust, were roused to motion again. She knew in those moments with him that she had been waiting a long time just to desire a man . . . to feel like a woman again.

She cautioned herself to stay calm in the storm of new awakening, because she felt his attraction to her, as well. She had to stay centered to earth.

Don't look at the sky. The stars were arrows, glistening, darting all around them. One could be struck so unexpectedly on a night like this. On a week like this, when everything in her life seemed somehow changed.

"Who . . ." she asked him weakly, her thoughts lingering on the memory of the night they met, "were you grieving for?"

"Huh?"

"When I first saw you in the library. You said you'd lost a friend."

He fell into a strained silence.

"Is it too painful to talk about?"

Keith swallowed. "I didn't mean to mislead you about that, Laura. I just didn't . . . I didn't feel like trying to explain it because I knew you caught me in tears that night. My manly pride was on the line."

"What are you talking about? What does pride have to do with grieving for a loved one who has died?"

His discomfort was made obvious by his hesitation. "The loved one," he said softly, not meeting her eyes, "was . . . was my dog."

"Your . . . ?" Laura's heart lurched in a surge of new understanding. The image of him in the library rushed back to her—blue-gray eyes shaded in sadness across a silent room, a fleeting expression of loneliness she hadn't translated until now.

The very thing he'd been hesitant to divulge—the reason for his grief—endeared him to her deeply. The warmth of her feelings would spill into her dreams. Laura knew this, and was beginning to accept it.

Gently she said, "Losing a pet you love is one of life's saddest experiences, Keith. Please don't say you thought I'd think less of you if I knew you were capable of grieving for a friend who happened to be nonhuman."

"Well, I didn't know you, then. It was too early in the evening. I felt responsible, in a way, because I brought him out here. He was sixteen years old, and the trip and the Tucson heat were too much for him. My daughter was pretty upset, since we'd had the dog all her life. I admit I was upset, too."

His eyes were accustomed to the dark now; he could see her in the shadows of evening. She shivered very slightly, yet the late-summer night was warm.

He reasoned that if she was not trembling from cold, then the reason had to be him. He was unsure how to interpret it. Maybe she was a little frightened of him.

"Laura," he whispered. "I have to go. I have a very early day tomorrow."

"Yes..." she nodded, thinking, *must you go so soon*? She smoothed back her hair and led him from the deck through the house to the front door where he took her hand. "Thank you for tonight."

"Thank you, Keith."

"I'd like to call you. Can I have your phone number?"

"Oh...sure...of course...I'll write it down for you."

She disappeared for a moment and came back with a small sheet of white paper. He folded it carefully and put it in his pocket.

"Good night, Laura. Sweet dreams."

"G'night. You too."

"Will you have dinner with me?"

"Yes. Of course."

"Day after tomorrow?"

She nodded.

He patted his pocket over the white sheet of paper to show he valued it highly. "I'll phone."

She stood at the doorway, watching him walk out into the little garden and through the iron gate. Only when she saw the headlights of his car swing around the curve of her drive and out onto the street did she close the front door.

Sighing deeply, happy and confused, she paced aimlessly through the house. Her deep-slumbering emotions had come awake so swiftly and bloomed so brightly that she was completely off balance.

Still pacing, caught in a web of dreams, Laura heard the crunch of wheels in her gravel drive. Her heart nearly stopped beating, then it began pounding wildly. She ran to the entry and turned on the outside lights. Keith was already inside the gate.

In the open doorway the soft night breezes rustled the silk of her blouse. She watched his approach, which was slow, a bit hesitant.

He reached for her hands and held them tightly.

"Did you forget something, Keith?"

"Yes. I forgot to kiss you good-night."

His grip on her hands slowly loosened. He reached for her, cupping her chin in his hands, lifting her face gently as he bent to kiss her. At the first touch of his lips, all strength left Laura and her legs no longer wanted to hold her weight. She leaned into him, accepting his kiss, feeling his heart pound against her breast.

Were these sensations forgotten? Or never before felt? Laura was unsure, except that her response to this man was one of acceptance. He had somehow felt that, somehow known. Just as she somehow had known with pounding heart why he had come back.

The touch of his lips was gentle, almost hesitant, lingering longer than he intended. His fingers moved from their feather touch on her cheeks and slid through her hair, caressing softly.

A new moment in time. New rustles of yearning from somewhere deep inside, a long time hidden. A sky shimmering with bright and unfamiliar stars. A moment to be long remembered and often relived.

He moved back slowly, still touching her hair, his gray-blue eyes lingering on hers. His voice was a husky whisper. "Good night, Laura."

"Good night . . ."

For the second time she watched his headlights circle the drive and disappear. But this time there was no pacing afterward. Laura walked back to the deck where she could see the spill of diamonds down in the valley below her and the bright new stars blinking in the sky above her. Lavender shadows of softly blowing palo verde leaves moved around her. The evening song of the desert held new melodies, music for the heart and for the blood. For a long time Laura stood alone, thinking new and unfamiliar thoughts, sweetly exciting thoughts, of the man whose touch lingered softly on her skin.

SPLENDID GARDENS extended from the restaurant terrace: green lawn, flower-embroidered ledges sloping
toward the desert, which rested below in the summer
dust. Still farther down, the lights of the valley flickered like a field of misplaced stars. A fountain sang in
colored lights near their table. During dinner they had
talked of many things—light things.

Now, over wine and cheese, Keith pressed Laura's
hand gently over the table. "You look lovely tonight.
Have I told you?"

"Yes," she said with a smile. "But I don't mind you
saying it again. Thank you. You look great yourself."

He grinned. "I've never been in a city as casual as
Tucson. I was told before I came that I could put my ties
away and forget them, and that's just what I've done.
Not that I had many to put away. I'm a slob by nature."

"If that's so, you hide it well. But it's true you won't
need your ties. I've seen jeans at the opera here."

"Opera? Do you enjoy opera?"

"Yes, very much. Do you?"

"I strongly doubt it. Opera wouldn't be my sort of
thing."

Laura smiled. "Somehow I guessed that. What about your daughter?"

His eyes shifted. "What about her?"

"You don't talk about her much. How is she adjusting to her new environment? What sort of activities does she like?"

"Tina? Oh, you know, the rock bands, clothes, boys..."

"Teenagers live in a culture of their own, I guess."

"Yeah. I guess."

Laura, he knew, could sense his hesitation to discuss his daughter, and so he made a great effort to be casual about it. He couldn't hide the fact that he didn't know Tina very well anymore, but this might be true for many parents of sixteen-year-olds. As Laura said, their cultures were very different, their interests were suddenly different. And so were their values. She would know about that.

What she wouldn't know about was the pressure on a parent who failed. Or the guilt, when the best you could do wasn't good enough and all your efforts backfired. She couldn't know the heartache of seeing your child in serious trouble unless she'd experienced it herself.

"Tina's adjusting okay," he lied. "At least she's doing her homework. She can get good grades when she wants to."

"I'm sure it always takes a little time. To make new friends and all."

"Yeah." He was conscious of the warmth of her hand. Conscious of the music in her voice and of the music of the splashing water in the nearby fountain. The cool of the desert night was so welcome after the heat of the day, and darkness welcome after the intense sun. "I don't suppose," he said, after a time of listening to the fountain, "that the desert is such a good place to take a hike at night."

"Not this time of year, not in this particular desert, without thick boots and good lights. Later, when the creepy crawlies are hibernating, you can hike up McGee Canyon on footpaths, as long as you can see well enough not to walk into a cactus."

"Tonight it's easy enough to see. I don't ever remember moonlight as bright as this."

"This is—" she looked at the sky "—a particularly beautiful night. Would you like to go back and sit on my terrace, or in the garden?"

"Since I don't have that kind of atmosphere to offer you, yes, I sure would."

On her terrace he sat back against yellow cushions with an arm around her, savoring the nearness of her. "Laura, can I ask you a personal question?"

"Sure."

"Is there a man, I mean, any special man, in your life?"

Her answer was surprisingly quick. "No. Does that surprise you?"

"Yes, frankly. A woman like you must be dodging men at every turn."

"On the contrary. I send out negative signals."

He paused on the edge of laughter. "Uh-uh. I don't agree with that . . ."

"Well . . . I don't send them out . . . to you. You're not other men though, are you?"

"No," he answered, huskiness beginning to color his voice. "I'm not other men."

Silence fell, but neither of them thought of it as silence. The very air around them was full of so many thoughts, feelings, and anticipations in the growing closeness between them that were so natural, so easy, so inevitable.

"You're rather a man of mystery," she said finally.

"Mystery? Hardly."

"Oh, yes. There are mysteries about you, many thoughts unspoken."

"My unspoken thoughts are of you."

"Are they? Why are they unspoken?"

He merely smiled at her, as if she already knew.

The smile caused her heart to lurch, because she did know. She knew from the way he looked at her across the table at dinner, admiringly, and with his concentration settled on her, oblivious to the fact that there were other people in the dining room. Even now, the soft pressure of his arm on her shoulders strengthened as he shifted closer. Anticipation of moments to come danced brightly on the wings of new awakening. Yes, she knew Keith's unspoken thoughts. And she had become aware of the shivers of her own thoughts at the nearness of him.

The scent of after-shave, the sweetness of his breath as he embraced her moved her to the total reality of the man who took her gently into his arms and bent to brush his lips against her cheek. She closed her eyes, better to feel the sensations of his lips, of the touch of his skin, the hint of the roughness of whiskers, although he was freshly shaven.

She was unable to hold back a sigh just before his lips moved over hers, very lightly at first, then deeper. She was aware of a strange kind of release of a tightness within her that had kept other men at a distance for so long. But she welcomed the closeness of this man, welcomed the scent of him and the soft sound of his breath and the taste of his lips. And she welcomed his thighs against hers, very lightly, as if he were so carefully aware of how he touched her.

Strength left her. Only the yielding to her emotion—to their emotions—remained. New yielding. New longing. So soon, so fast! No, it wasn't soon, not really, for she had thought of Keith Martin almost constantly since she had first set eyes on him, since the first moment she had heard his voice. How strange it felt, yielding to the pull toward wild, runaway emotions. Toward anticipation of knowing Keith better and better, of being closer and closer to him. Of being part of his days, and of his nights.

Shocked at the depths and heights of her own desire, Laura pulled slightly away.

His arms released their hold. "I got a little carried away just now . . . lost in the . . . in your kiss, Laura . . ."

"Yes," she breathed. "Yes . . . so did I . . ."

"I know." His eyes were soft as his hands moved to her cheeks. For a time he studied her. "You overwhelm me. I've never in my life been so overwhelmed by anyone."

The white moonlight reflected the shine of his eyes, muted and smoothed the features of his face—incredibly handsome features. His thick hair fell over his forehead in loose curls.

She reached up to touch his hair. "I'm overwhelmed myself . . . by you, by my . . . by . . ."

"By how I make you feel?"

She nodded.

He stroked her cheek, looking into her eyes. "If it were your beauty alone, I'd have enough to deal with. But it's more. It's everything. Your smile, your voice, your eyes... I'm helpless to hide my feelings from you."

"Do you want to do that?"

He hesitated. "It seems I should, because it's . . . because we haven't known each other very long. I'm trying to be proper. In one way I don't know you very well, but in another I feel I've known you forever. Does that make sense?"

"Perfect sense. I'm not doing well at hiding my feelings from you, either."

"No, you're not. They're in your eyes, and in your kiss. Isn't that all right?"

She was frightened. "I don't know. I feel . . ." She didn't want to say it.

But he knew. "Vulnerable?"

"You're a very astute and sensitive man, Keith."

"I'm not astute, and usually not sensitive at all. With you it's different."

His fingers warm on her face, his eyes on hers, prolonged the helplessness she felt to control her own emotions. "Why different with me?"

"Because I care how you feel...."

"Keith...I—"

His kiss interrupted her. It was the kiss of a man she knew and did not know, of a man she wanted to know, wanted to be close to, close and closer. He opened his lips over hers, moving his body against hers.

The once cool moonlight seemed to heat and burn. The once icy stars turned to fires in the sky. Once peaceful sighs became harder breaths of asking and of answering.

The kiss lasted until the stars, too, burned. "Laura," he whispered, "we have to keep talking."

"Yes," she murmured, moving her hands from his neck to his arms.

"Conversation..." he pleaded, his lips touching her forehead. "Please distract me..."

She blinked. He was right. It would be so easy to forget to talk in these bold new moments of recognizing what they were not yet ready to assimilate. Of discovering their fascination each for the other. He sensed her fear of feelings held so long at bay, and she knew it.

For her sake, he drew slowly from the embrace whispering, "Laura, I think I ought to go."

"Yes . . ." she breathed, disappointed and grateful at the same time. His earlier suggestion of trying a diversion of conversation had been already dismissed as an impotent idea. The vibrations between them were just too strong.

He stood up as if he were afraid he'd change his mind unless he acted swiftly. "I don't want to leave, but . . ."

"I know . . ." she said softly. "I need some time, Keith . . ."

"Yeah. I'm aware of that."

"Thank you for that." It was eerie, his tuning in to her feelings better than she herself could grasp them. Much as she hated for him to leave, she was experiencing also a hollow relief, for her emotions had taken flight and soared out of any familiar range, demanding their freedom. She had hoped it might happen someday, but now that her heart-thoughts could once again fly free, Keith was giving her a chance to catch up with them. He wouldn't say so. Chances were he wouldn't be able to express it, even if he tried, yet he seemed to understand her. A deeper level of communication was forming between them.

She took his hand in silence and walked with him through the house to her front door.

He stopped only long enough for a good-night kiss, after which he whispered, "Are you free on Friday night?"

"Yes." She had no idea whether she had something on her calendar for Friday night.

"Great. Maybe we'll be in the mood for a movie or something. I'll give you a call." He squeezed her hand. "G'night, Laura."

"Good night."

She returned to the terrace after Keith had left and sat down to finish her glass of wine. How would she sleep tonight, with her mind whirling like this? How could she still her tumbling thoughts long enough to rest? The heat of his lips lingered on hers, the scent of his after-shave remained, the press of his body still seemed to be gentle against her.

She felt alive again, as she had so often fantasized she would, when love came back into her life, when dreams became real. When a man she'd known only in imagination became a person she could touch. Maybe she hadn't really believed a man for her existed. She hadn't looked because she hadn't known she was ready to find him. Or maybe she'd been too afraid.

She wasn't afraid now. The wonderful feelings of being truly alive—all those feelings she'd wanted back—were very, very welcome.

5

By THE TIME Keith and Laura returned to her house after a leisurely dinner and a movie, it was raining hard.

"Looks like we won't be having a drink on the terrace tonight," she observed. "Pull up next to my car in the carport, Keith, and we'll dash in the back door."

Inside he asked, "Isn't all this rain unusual for the desert?"

"No. This is our monsoon season. Traditionally the rains are supposed to begin to let up by late August, but the past two years the rainy season has come later and lasted much longer—even into October. It looks as if it'll be the same again this year."

"It's refreshingly cool, even though we are stuck inside tonight."

Laura set her handbag on the counter. "You're soaked from going after the car in the parking lot. We should've parked nearer the theater."

"I didn't realize how hard it was raining."

"You're drenched from head to—" She gazed at his sneakers in amazement and leaned down for a closer look. "Keith! Your shoelaces! *Snoopy* shoelaces?"

His grin was mischievous. "Like my Snoopys?"

"Yes! Did you actually buy them?"

"Sure."

Laura shook her head, smiling. "There's a side to you I don't know yet, isn't there?"

" 'Yet' is a word full of promise."

Their eyes met and held. How strangely incongruous, she thought, for a man as burly as Keith to be wearing comic shoelaces. It demonstrated his sense of humor. But more, it was yet another statement of how secure he was in his own manhood. It wouldn't matter much what he wore; he exuded an air of that kind of toughness men understood and feared, and women stood in awe of. The effect was especially potent when the physical touch of such a man, offered in gentle moments, could be so surprisingly tender. . . .

She smiled up at him. "All your little Snoopys are sopping wet. You ought to take them off. There are plenty of towels in the bathroom if you want to try to dry off a bit. Meantime, I'll fix us something to drink. What would you like?"

"I don't care. Whatever you're in the mood for."

"A little Amaretto over ice?"

"Sounds fine."

The drinks were on the table. She was returning to the living room carrying a dish of cashews when he came into the room barefoot and wearing no shirt.

"Hope you'll excuse my state of undress. I hate wet clothes."

Laura was taken off guard by the sight of him standing in the soft light of the room in nothing but a pair of snug-fitting Levi's. His broad shoulders, his deeply tanned chest shadowed by dark hair, his muscular arms might have belonged to a model on the pages of a magazine—one of those virile males posing on a horse or in front of a construction site. Untamed, dark and unnervingly sexy, this man wore many reminders of his strange, rough past.

"Of course I don't mind," she said. "You look terrific in your...state of undress." She set the dish on the glass table. "You must swim a lot. You're so tanned."

"I usually do a few laps after work. It doesn't take long to tan down here in the south. You're—" He stroked her arm. "You're not very tanned for an Arizona lady."

"The sun-baking days of my youth are over. There are too many warnings about danger to the skin."

"Such lovely skin . . ." he murmured, now brushing her smooth upper arm.

She felt little shivers at his touch and an uncontrollable urge to reach for him, to touch him, too, which would have been natural enough had he been dressed. But as he was, her action was bolder. Her hand lay on his wide, cool, bare shoulder. His arms encircled her then, hugging her, holding her tightly against his chest. He said nothing, only held her while Laura responded with her heart and her arms, leaning into him, holding on to him tightly.

The stereo tape she had switched on a few moments before sent sweet strains of music through the room. Rain pounded on the roof. For a long time they stood silent in each other's arms with the sounds of the music and the rain and the beating of their hearts.

"Laura," he whispered finally. "I've thought of you... I can't keep my mind off you."

"I've thought of you, too. Times when I..." Her voice was muffled against his bare shoulder.

"I know..." he whispered. "Yeah, I know."

His hands moved along her back, to her neck and through her hair. She lifted her eyes to him in response to his silent signal, lifted her eyes and her lips to meet those she had longed for in the quiet hours of the night.

A kiss begun softly began to rush through her head like the rapids of a stream—emotions roaring and tumbling, raging, building to unfathomable heights. The kiss became another and another, breaths as wild and hard as the pounding rain above them.

Her hands moved over his back as she absorbed the feel of his skin, so cool at first, becoming warmer with the passing seconds. Leaning into his body, she was aware of the movement of his chest, of the dampness of his rain-splashed jeans penetrating her thin cotton shirt, of the physical wakening of his passion.

His lips were touching her throat now. She leaned back against the support of his arm, eyes closed, accepting his desire for her, accepting her own desire... for him.

He whispered her name several times, sighing finally. "Your name is like music, Laura. Your skin—" He was brushing his lips over her shoulder now, sliding the tiny strap of her sun top down. "Your skin is so soft...."

His lips moved lower; his hand caressed her breast over the fabric of her blouse. At the press of his fingers to her breast, the last of her shrinking inhibitions left her and steadily mounting desire soared until she almost ached with it.

"Keith," she whispered. "Your jeans . . . they're so wet. . . ."

He was kissing her throat again, one hand behind her back to support her, the other on her breast. "And they're damned uncomfortable," he mumbled. "You wouldn't mind if I took them off?"

She smiled, her eyes filled with fire and mischief and newly roused desire. Her smile was the answer to his question . . . to all his questions.

One hand moved to the button of his jeans. He smiled slowly.

She took a step back and turned toward the table where she had set down the glasses of Amaretto. "Do you . . . ah . . . want your drink?"

"You and the night are all I need, Laura."

She heard the small rip of his zipper. When she turned back, a stemmed glass in each hand, he was tugging down the jeans. They were wetter than he'd realized and were resisting. The right side of the band of his low-waisted briefs caught with the denim. He pulled it back into place, but when the other side caught, he muttered a soft "To hell with it" and allowed them to slide off with his jeans. In the time it took Laura to begin breathing again, he was standing naked before her.

She stood motionless, holding the glasses out in front of her, a trembling sensation in the pit of her stomach. Keith was so tanned, so beautifully built, so strongly muscled, so insouciantly at ease without clothes that his nakedness was less an astonishment to her than it was pure pleasure.

Unashamed eyes admired his body as he moved forward, accepted one of the glasses and gulped back the dark liquid in one giant swallow. She raised the other glass to her lips with trembling fingers, took only a small sip to make sure she wouldn't choke and set the little goblet down again as his arms moved around her and his lips once again found hers.

The gentle press of his body was different now; there was no longer the barrier of his jeans, and her cotton skirt was very thin. And wherever he touched her, she was throbbing. Deep into his hungry kiss her heartbeats tangled with the taste of his tongue on hers, her hands strayed in sensuous circles over the small of his back to his buttocks. He moved closer then, his own hands responding by urging her against him.

"Laura . . . let me know you . . . touch you . . . let me love you. . . ."

She knew that in making a claim to her heart, he was asking her to trust him. "Yes . . ." she murmured.

His response was another kiss. Soft against her lips, then her throat, her shoulder, her breasts, over her blouse. Then he was kneeling before her and running his hands up and down her smooth, bare legs, under her skirt, caressing her thighs, her hips, her stomach.

Catching the elastic top of her lace panties, he removed them slowly while touching her, uttering words like *treasure* and *beauty*. She stood trembling in the wake of his gentle explorations until her knees threatened to buckle.

Laura knelt, facing him in silence that did not seem to be silence, allowing him to unbutton her blouse and slide the small garment from her shoulders. She watched only his eyes, not his hands, as he unhooked her bra and let it fall away. Still watching his eyes as he touched her breasts for the first time, she heard murmurs of his praise and his heightening passion. Hands so big, so warm, holding her, lifting her softness to his lips.

Her fingers in his thick, dark hair, she held his head against her breasts, drowning in the sensations he could give her with his lips and his tongue.

Presently he murmured, "Laura . . . you're trembling so. . . ." And with arms on her shoulders, he urged her down onto the plush white carpet and lay beside her, tenderly touching her face. "I want to please you, Laura. But just seeing you, touching you, is making me crazy. This time—this first time—I don't know how long I'm going to last."

She reached up to him, placing her fingers on his lips. "Why do you think I'm trembling? It's all right, Keith . . . I'll be with you."

He raised himself to his knees and lifted Laura's pale blue skirt up over her waist. Lying against the white carpet, looking up at him, she watched the heaving of his broad chest while he sought new intimacy. His eyes, his hands, were taking. Asking for more. Asking for everything.

She moaned, unable to lie still, unable to control her responses or her wild need, compelled to share with him the joy and the fulfillment he and no other man could give her. *No other man*, she thought dizzily in the great high winds of passion. Only this man. Of all the men she knew or had ever known, she wanted only this man.

When his warm body moved over hers she closed her eyes in anticipation, then opened them again and looked up at his face. His hands clasped hers above her head and her response was a spontaneous, acquiescent shifting of her knees, for him. She heard her name in his husky whisper and grasped his hands tightly, then tighter.

"Keith . . ." she breathed, his strength and his power filling her. Their bodies merged in a rush and a flood of love.

His chest moving with great breaths, Keith rolled his weight away from her and lay beside her, his arm around her waist. Laura turned toward him, resting her hand on his upper arm, lightly caressing the bulging muscles.

After a time he heaved a ragged sigh. "You're a miracle! I've never wanted a woman the way I've wanted you. I never thought this would happen to me."

She waited for her breath to return, for the world to return to normal, knowing it never would. Her life was changed. Nothing would be the same, ever again. "I never thought it would happen to me, either."

He brushed wisps of hair from her eyes. "I didn't plan for this tonight. I had very noble ideas about waiting to be certain you were ready. You know, sort of working up to it gradually. I was out of my mind thinking I had the willpower to resist you."

She smiled dreamily. "Is that why we're here . . . on the floor?"

"I wasn't even aware of where we were, except that we were together."

A surge of joy welled up in her. The word *together* had a new meaning now. So many words had new meanings. *Tonight* was a weave of indelible memories, and the word *tomorrow* meant far different things than it had ever meant before.

They lay quietly for a long time; Keith seemed to be dozing. Eventually the fabric of the thick, soft carpet against her skin was beginning to itch. Gently she pulled out from under his arm.

When she stood up, her crumpled blue skirt fell around her knees. Soundlessly she went into the bathroom, and then to her bedroom where she stepped out of the wrinkled skirt and slid into a thin lavender satin robe. The feel of Keith, the vapors of his body, remained with her. She wanted the feel of him to last forever.

He had rolled onto his back when she returned to the living room. His eyes were still closed, his arms and legs sprawled apart, skin dark against the white of the carpet. She stood over him, admiring the beauty of him, aching, almost hurting to touch him.

He opened his eyes and looked up at her with a soft, dreamy expression.

"Were you asleep?" she asked.

"I don't think so. I was lying here listening to the rain."

"Yes. It's a beautiful rain."

Keith sat up lazily, brushing his hair from his eyes. "Do you like the rain?"

"I love it. During the winter, when it almost never rains, I sometimes long for dark skies and this lovely sound on the roof."

"Let's make the most of it, then." He rose and took her hand. "Let's go."

He led her to the glass doors that opened onto the terrace, then paused before sliding them open. "Okay?"

"Sure, why not?"

He untied the belt of her satin robe and slipped it from her shoulders, letting it fall onto the carpet. A thrill of excitement shot through her; she had never stood naked in the rain.

The first splashes were very cold—tiny sparks of electricity on already-fevered flesh. Rain in autumn: false spring filled with the vitality of real spring. Raindrops glittering in soft light that shone through glass doors, washing all inhibitions away. He held her close until their bodies were too wet to feel the shock of the cold. Then his hands began to slide smoothly over her shoulders and her throat and her breasts, his kisses following. Warm lips against her cold, wet skin.

Warm lips finding hers, opening over hers, started her heart beating wildly. The intensity of his kiss brought changes to his body, which she could feel against her; it brought changes to her own body, too. And the kiss lingered, prolonged, until they were moving together. Her small moans were lost in the beat of the splashing rain.

The light from the house seemed to grow brighter over the terrace as their eyes adjusted to the night. White light misted by the rain. He drew back slightly and looked down at her; the rain splashed in her eyes. "Laura," he said softly. "I love you. There's no doubt left in me. I love you."

She felt the sting that precedes tears, and then the warmth of those tears in her eyes. Tears mingling with rain. Words stuck in her throat—words caught in a seizure of joy.

Somehow, in shadows of darkness and rain, he had seen her tears. To her wonder, he saw them and kissed her eyes. He tasted the salt of her tears then.

"Laura?"

Her arms circled tightly around his bare back. "Oh, Keith! I love you, too."

"Why was I so lucky to find you? I've never been this lucky."

"Nor I. It's destiny. I felt a strange little spark the first time I saw you."

"Why are you crying, Laura?"

"I don't know. It's just that you make me so happy."
She smiled up at him. Sparkles of water splashed his
face. "Have you ever stood naked in the rain before?"

He laughed. "No. Definitely not. Have you?"

"No. And it feels wonderful."

"You feel wonderful."

"So do you."

"You can feel how much I want you."

"Yes . . ."

"Again . . ."

"Yes . . ." Her hand moved slowly down over his hips,
bold explorations around to the hard muscles of his
abdomen.

He groaned softly at her touch. "Maybe we . . . maybe
it's time to go inside. We could continue this in the rain,
but I don't want you to get too chilled."

"Let's go in the side door. There are towels in the
utility room."

With the towel she handed to him, fresh from the
dryer, Keith began to dry Laura's body, her back and
chest, her arms. Still dripping wet himself, he knelt on
the floor in a puddle to dry her legs.

"Aren't you awfully cold, Keith?"

"Are you kidding? I'm burning with passion."

She smiled and threw a towel over his shoulders.
Wrapped in a towel herself, she led him through the
kitchen and living room and into her bedroom and
drew back the bedspread. Giving her some private
time, Keith excused himself and found her bathroom.

She was sitting on the edge of the bed, vigorously rubbing her wet hair with a towel, when he returned. He took the towel from her gently and lay on the bed, pulling her down next to him.

"Now," he said. "Will you continue?"

She hesitated a moment in a small attack of shyness, here in the light of the bedroom.

"You were touching me, Laura."

The huskiness of his voice, the gentle press of his hand against her breast brought back the spell. With it came the longing of before, the desire to know his body as well as he knew it himself. And now, by invitation . . .

There was new ease in his urging. Thresholds of fierce, long-hidden dreams borne on a night filled with rain, a night filled with love. Fire within her fingers, fire against her cheek, fire upon her lips. Fire that was Keith's passion, flaming with her own. Her turn for giving, his for taking.

"Tell me how to please you. . . ."

His voice was jerky, almost a moan. "You are . . . pleasing me . . . Laura . . ."

"But tell me . . ."

"You know already . . ." His eyes closed. "Oh, honey . . . you know!"

She found his submission to her overwhelming. At first he had sensed her shyness. How quickly and skillfully he was making her forget it was ever there! *Accept your power over me*, he was saying in a thousand ways. And in the fires fanned by her touch, she did, willingly, accept.

Her cheek against him felt the perspiration forming on his body. She tasted the salt of his skin. "Keith, should I . . . ?"

His breath quickened. He closed his eyes. "Anything. Anything you want . . . to do. Everything you want to do . . ."

Her unleashed passion guided her to horizons of love she had never discovered, until Keith. Laura was caught helplessly in the web of magic this passion had spun around them; she was caught so helplessly that she forgot there was a world outside this room, or even darkness, or rain.

"This . . . ?"

His voice was breath only. "Oh . . . don't . . . stop . . . don't . . ."

Then there was only the sound of rain on the roof, the sound of her own pounding heart and of Keith's erratic breathing. Sounds of the senses finding unity in extravagant, unlimited freedom. Until from the whirl of time his breath became a deep moan, so deep that it startled her.

"Now, Laura! Come to me . . . to my arms . . . I want you with me!" A fevered shudder silenced him.

Trembling, he reached for her. To take her to him, with him, to take the lead again and carry her to a place beyond the darkened hush of night, past all yesterdays, above the rustle of the crumpled pillows, toward the top of the world.

He stayed with her until her body quaked out of control, out of the sphere that was earth, this quiet bedroom. He cried out, releasing her name with the flooding rivers of his passion, as if a dam had broken and let his soul go free.

6

HABITUALLY UNORGANIZED, Keith would make the hurried decision every day on his way home from work as to whether he and Tina would go out for dinner or eat at home. Every time he opted to cook at home, he would stand in a long line at the supermarket checkout and swear he would never shop at that time of day again. But old habits died hard. Here he was in the market again, at five o'clock in the afternoon.

Today the decision had been easy. He had to get something Tina could fix for herself at home since he was going out to dinner. Again. She was getting sensitive about his evenings away; he hadn't mentioned at breakfast that he would be out tonight; now he wished he had.

The door of their apartment was unlocked, immediate evidence that Tina was home from school. Books were strewn over the dining table, tennis shoes lay in the middle of the floor and glasses of melting ice and cola sat on the kitchen counter. As she wasn't in the apartment, he knew she had to be either at Kim's or the pool.

He quickly put away the groceries and set still-wrapped daisies in a glass of water. He looked at his

watch and went to his bedroom to change into swim
trunks. A few laps in the pool would be refreshing after the heat of the late-summer day; swimming after
work was becoming a habit.

A glance into his daughter's bedroom made him
cringe. Clothes were piled on the floor and on the bed,
walls were covered with posters of rock stars. As usual,
he just looked away, thinking he himself had always
been a bad example as far as neatness was concerned.
Life was crammed with more important things to worry
about. In about a week they'd have another cleanup
Saturday and get the apartment in shape. In the meantime, Tina was responsible for doing her own laundry,
and she was getting better about accepting that responsibility. In fact, she had become extremely metic-
ulous in her personal grooming. Her dresser tops, once
piled with Barbie Doll clothes and stuffed animals were
overflowing now with cosmetics and exotic-looking
bottles. It remained a great mystery to him how the
changes had all come about so fast. Too fast. Now he
barely knew her.

On his walks to and from the swimming pool,
through natural cactus gardens, Keith was becoming
familiar with the flora of the desert. Today as he slapped
along the path in yellow rubber thongs, he wondered
about telling Tina he was having dinner with Laura.
He'd never mentioned Laura for the simple reason that
he had fallen in love—deeply in love—with her, and
Tina would sense it. She would sense it and deeply resent it, out of jealousy and fear of losing him. There

would be a terrible scene. He would put off telling Tina about Laura for still another day; he wasn't in the mood for a confrontation.

The sight of Tina lying on her towel on the grass by the pool should have reassured him that her reactions might be changing as she matured. It didn't. As always lately, he was less reassured than shocked by her metamorphosis from child to woman. Deeply tanned, wearing a revealing white swimsuit, Tina was slim and tall and beautiful by any standards. She could easily pass for eighteen. It worried Keith that Tina was beginning to realize her beauty. He had been so helpless to stop her rebellion against the standards of society, and he had no idea how far that rebellion was going to go. Maybe the counseling would help, but he had little faith in it.

Tina and Kim didn't see him approach, but he was aware that everyone else at the pool did. Keith could feel eyes on him as he walked to the far side of the pool. He was used to the admiration of women and sometimes he was flattered by it, but today his mind was elsewhere.

Tina's friend Kim, looking up from a magazine, greeted him enthusiastically as he threw his towel on the grass. His daughter, wearing headphones, raised a hand in recognition of his presence, her head nodding in rhythm to a tune she could hear and he, to his relief, could not.

Feeling like an intruder in their strange and private world, Keith merely smiled, set his sunglasses on the towel and dived into the pool, welcoming the cold of the water. He swam vigorously back and forth until he was out of breath and had to slow his powerful strokes.

When he climbed out, panting slightly, an attractive, dark-haired woman in a flowered one-piece suit was sitting beside his towel, arms across her knees, watching him. She handed him up the towel, smiling.

"I'm Marybeth Cotter, Kim's mother. I've been anxious to meet you."

Drying his face and arms, he returned her smile and sat down on the grass. "I feel I know you already from all our phone conversations." He knew a little about her—that she was a divorcee and had recently moved to Tucson from California. A few days ago, on the phone, she'd invited him for coffee, but he'd been very busy with paperwork at the time and eager to meet Laura later.

His daughter pulled off her headphones and brushed her fingers through her still-damp dark hair. Her brown eyes were hidden behind sunglasses. "Hey, Dad, Kim and I have massive homework in algebra. We were just saying, like, we could do it at her house and me spend the night. Her mom says it's okay if it's okay with you."

"It seems," Keith said to Marybeth Cotter, "that Tina is at your house more than her own."

"It's fine with me. I'm glad for Kim to have the company. The girls get along so well."

"It's a school night," he reminded Tina.

"What's the major prob with that, Dad? We won't stay up too late."

"Don't worry. I'll see they don't," Marybeth said. "In fact, the girls would like to fix some hamburgers for dinner. Will you join us?"

The invitation caught him off guard. "Thanks, but I can't tonight. I've made other plans."

"Cool, Dad," Tina said sarcastically. Her pout lingered for some moments, then quickly disappeared. It struck him that, having thought about it, she probably welcomed the excuse not to have to discuss today's counseling session with him.

He sighed. Everything seemed to be going all right with the counseling, if he could judge from Tina's attitude. She complained about her therapist in an offhand way, but the fact that she didn't balk at keeping her appointments encouraged him. There were even moments lately when she seemed her old cheerful self, the way she'd been when she was a little girl.

He had stepped out of the shower and was in the kitchen wearing only a towel around his waist when Tina and Kim came into the apartment chattering and laughing, accompanied by the radio music that seemed to follow them everywhere.

Kim, a petite blonde, smiled at him. "Hey, what are the flowers for?"

Tina was carrying in a load of books from the dining room. She set them on the counter and eyed her father strangely. Her gaze moved to the bouquet of soft white daisies in the glass jar on the counter. "Are those flowers for me, Dad? I mean, like, you wouldn't buy them for *you*, would you? Is it, like, some special day or something?"

"It's not a special day. They were there by the market checkout. I stopped to buy some groceries for you tonight. There's cola and chips if you and Kim want to take them over there."

This wasn't the right time, here in front of Kim, to mention the fact that he had a dinner date with a woman for whom he had, on impulse, picked up a little bunch of fresh daisies. Tina knew him too well. It wasn't like him to buy flowers. She was immediately suspicious. What with all his recent evenings away from home, she was beginning to put it all together. He couldn't put off telling her about Laura too much longer. It was a matter of figuring out how to tell her. That the news might contribute to her rebelliousness worried him.

"They're neat, Dad! I adore flowers! Can I take them to Kim's? Like, I mean, nobody will enjoy them over here in the kitchen, will they?" She had picked up the bouquet and was burying her nose in the flowers.

He smiled with a shrug. "Why not? Take them, if you like them that much."

She gave him her most radiant smile, one he had a hard time interpreting. "I'll be back in the morning to get dressed for school. Will you be here?"

"Of course I'll be here; aren't I always? I'll see you in the morning." He kissed her forehead.

Tina, still smiling happily, reached for the bouquet of daisies in the jar.

THEY WERE HAPPY TIMES for him—these long evenings with Laura, in the rush and warmth of new love—perhaps the happiest of his life. The moments were notes of music that formed a symphony whenever she was near him. Her voice, her movements, all music, all consumed with her love for him. It was too easy to forget everything else but her touch. Her laughter. Her body soft against his.

Foolishly or not, he did forget everything else. Love, he discovered, had that power over him. Laura was that power. Laura was love that had eluded him all his life, until now. The timing was bad, very bad. In this, his daughter's most difficult year, Keith didn't feel free to love. Yet he did love Laura, more deeply every day.

They explored their new love together, as they explored the desert together. It was all new to him—the dazzling, unforgettable sunsets and soft night breezes carrying the fragrances of the blooming desert.

"The silence is unlike anything I've ever heard," he said to her as they stood in the blue-black air on a night when the moon was new.

"Is it really?" she asked softly, taking his hand. "You've been to remote parts of Africa, haven't you? Where there isn't a town within a thousand miles?"

"Yes, but the night isn't silent like this, because the animals are so noisy."

"The night hunters here are very quiet in their travels—what few hunters there are. It must be wonderful to know other places, such faraway places. I've lived in Arizona all my life and never traveled anywhere."

"Is there any reason why you haven't traveled?"

"No. Well, there was never the time, I guess. When I was going to school I couldn't afford it, and later I was trying to establish my practice. . . ."

"Yeah," he said, understanding, while he imagined how it would be to travel the world with her. He had an image of them standing beside a pyramid, looking up, shading their eyes to the Egyptian sun. "I haven't, either. Traveled much, I mean. There was one trip to the Kenyan fossil fields, but I stayed only a few weeks because Tina had to get back to school."

"Tina was with you in Kenya?"

He nodded. "She enjoyed it for a while, but then it got pretty boring for her. She was only eleven . . ."

They were strolling in the desert acre that surrounded Laura's home, on a path she had cleared especially for night walks. Carefully marked with stones and cleared of overhanging cat-claw branches, the path was wide enough for two people, but it dead-ended after only a hundred feet. Just taking one step off the path in the dark was to risk catching painful thorns from the dense tangle of hostile desert growth.

Their flashlight beamed on a hopping shadow and Laura squeezed his arm. "Oh, look, Keith, a Colorado River toad! Such a big one! They only come out during the rainy season."

The brown toad sat perfectly still for a time on the warm, white sand, before it hopped out of the light beam. A short distance away a jackrabbit leaped up suddenly, startling them into laughter.

"Did you check out those incredible ears, Keith? I see that particular rabbit often. I call him Casper because he makes me think of a little ghost—always leaping out from behind something when I least expect it. Like now."

"You're a marvel, Laura. How many women would find so much beauty and joy in all these strange creatures?"

She laughed softly. "I find that everything is beautiful in its natural environment. The toad, the rabbit—they're all part of the whole."

"This is your natural environment, too, my love. The more I know you, the more I realize you, too, are a child of the desert. How many people feel the kind of love for it that you feel?"

"More than you'd imagine. My mother has always loved it and she taught me a great deal. The desert can be so hostile, you know. She made me realize that by respecting it, I would fear it less."

"You lived in the country?"

"A very tiny town. I once had a pet duckling killed by a scorpion, and I hated scorpions with a vengeance. I was terrified of them. But my mother tried to change that. She wanted me to look at all the strange desert inhabitants in perspective, to understand how everything had its place in the scheme of things. I was enchanted by her story of how all the ugly and poisonous creatures were refused a home by the forests and mountains, but were welcomed by the desert."

"I'd like to meet your mother."

"She lives in Mesa now. Maybe we can visit her sometime."

"Let's do that."

"You'd really like to meet my mother?"

"Very much."

Keith's feelings surprised even him. He really did want to meet Laura's mother, to become acquainted with another part of Laura's life. He wanted to understand her—her love of life, her love of the world around her. She was intriguing, and special. Unique. Laura was gentleness, softness. He'd known so little of either in his life. He'd never known he yearned so deeply for these things, till now.

"I'm glad you want to meet my mother." She squeezed his arm affectionately. "I've told her about you, you know."

"What did you tell her?"

"That you make me feel alive again. That being with you makes me very, very happy."

"I hope you added that the feeling's mutual."

"Yes," she answered softly. "I did add that."

Laura turned out the flashlight, handed it to him and took a blacklight from her bag. She began shining it over the desert floor.

"What's this?" he asked. "What the devil are you looking for with a blacklight?"

"It's a surprise. You'll see."

They walked in silence for a time, until Laura held the light beam steady and exclaimed, "There! Look, Keith!"

On the shadowy sand a few feet from the path was a large scorpion, shining iridescent in the blacklight. It was moving slowly, its tail down, unthreatened.

"I'll be damned! Scorpions glow in the dark?"

"They glow under black light. Isn't it amazing?"

"Amazing and eerie!" He gazed at the shining creature in fascination. "If you keep a blacklight on hand to search for these things at night, you've obviously conquered your fear of scorpions."

"Not entirely. I can accept them out here, doing whatever it is scorpions are supposed to do, but I really hate it when they get into the house. Once in a while one will show up on my ceiling or somewhere, and I'm not terribly proud of my reactions then, I'll admit. You wouldn't believe how fast they can run when they want to."

They watched the moving iridescence until it disappeared under the protection of a fallen prickly pear leaf.

"I'm glad I talked you into going on a night walk with me," Keith said with a smile.

"You couldn't have talked me into it except for this path. In hot weather the rattlesnakes like to come out at night." She laughed. "Trying to run from snakes, we'd be pin cushions in no time."

"A sobering thought. The jumping cactus hurts like hell. I learned that my first day in Tucson."

"Chollas. They're called chollas."

"I'll bet they've been called plenty of other things, as well, and more than a few by me. Is this the end of your path already?"

"I told you it was short."

They turned back, Keith shining the flashlight into the desert. A centipede slithered in and out of the beam; otherwise, the walk back was uneventful.

At the top of the slope, they entered the oasis of Laura's backyard. The pool shimmered silver blue with its underwater light. A light breeze rustled the branches of the palm tree overhead.

"It's beautiful," he said, when they were standing at the pool edge.

"Do you want to go for a swim?"

"Sure."

"Last one in is a lizard!" Laura challenged, kicking off her sandals and beginning to unbutton her blouse.

The odds were uneven because Keith was wearing sneakers and socks. She had dived into the pool and was swimming to the shallow end before he was out of his jeans. A powerful swimmer, he caught up with her and raced her back toward the diving board.

Laura was completely out of breath before she reached the shallow water once again, far behind Keith in the race. This time he stopped and waited for her, and she came into his arms panting.

"I . . . didn't have a . . . chance . . . in that race . . . and I thought I was . . . a fast swimmer . . ."

"I guess lizards are faster."

Under the water he began to caress her—flesh against naked flesh, wet and cool, and she responded by wrapping her legs around him, letting him hold her up while he kissed her. Their bodies heated with the warmth of the kiss, until the fire and ache of their passion overcame them. And in the soft silence of the desert night, they surrendered to the pure and simple beauty of their love.

JUSTINE MARTIN sat slumped in the overstuffed chair in Laura's office, her slender legs stretched in front of her, arms dangling over the sides of the chair. She wore slim blue jeans and a large shirt pulled in below the waist by a wide pink belt. She was barefoot. Both leather thongs had been kicked aside.

"My dad's got a new lover," she muttered, looking at the floor and not at her therapist. "It's like... you know... his same act over and over."

Laura sat across from her sixteen-year-old client, leaning back in her swivel chair. "Women?"

The girl scowled and nodded, still looking at the floor.

"Did he tell you he has this new... lover?"

"Well, like, he didn't have to. He bought her flowers." She looked up and smiled. "I, like, stole them, though."

"You stole the flowers?"

"Why not? I saw them and it was, like, oh, yeah, sure, when would he ever buy flowers for me? So I go, 'Hey, cool, Dad. You got me flowers,' and he goes, 'I didn't know you liked flowers.'"

"Did he tell you they were for someone else?"

"He was too chicken. He goes, 'Well, they were just there at the counter,' you know."

"He gave them to you?"

"Not exactly. I just, like, took them."

"But he didn't object?"

Justine shrugged.

"It's possible you were wrong, isn't it? That he did buy them for you?"

"My dad? No way! Like, he's just not the flowers type."

Laura sat thoughtfully for a time. "Do you think your father shouldn't see any women?"

"Well. It's, like, maybe I think he should learn. I mean, my mother left us. Then he married that bitch who hated my guts. He could, you know, go out and get sex if that's what he thinks he has to do . . . well, I mean, like, since men think it's real radical if they don't get it, like, every five minutes. . . ."

Inwardly Laura cringed. She had learned, though, not to reveal her reactions to anything her clients said. She reminded herself that, after all, Justine Martin was mild compared to some of the kids she'd interviewed.

"But if he buys a woman flowers it means he may think more of her than—"

"Yeah, than just the sex."

"And that's threatening to you."

The girl looked up and scowled once more, then looked down again in silence.

"Do you and your dad ever discuss his profession, Justine? Do you know much about what private detectives do?"

"I know it's, you know, late hours, so naturally he's hardly ever home and stuff."

"Does he ever discuss his cases with you?"

"No. It's detective stuff. Like, confidential. Everybody knows that."

"So confidential he doesn't even have an office?"

"He doesn't need one. He works . . . I mean, well, he has like an office at home. . . ." She shifted in the chair but didn't straighten. "I know what you're getting at. You think he might be into like illegal stuff. Yeah, right, since he has a criminal for a daughter and all."

"I wasn't thinking anything remotely like that," Laura answered. But she had wondered and wondered still why the girl was so evasive about her father's profession. Something was wrong; she just wasn't sure what.

Either the man was, as Justine suggested, into something illegal, or Justine wasn't telling the truth about the fact that he was a detective. Laura had run into this before. Kids who tried to keep as much of their private lives as secret as possible, thinking it might prevent a therapist from communication with the parents. Or it could be that the father was lying to Justine about what he did, and the girl suspected he was lying.

Little things didn't add up. In one breath Justine would describe an uncaring father who was never at home, and in the next she would unwittingly reveal something about him that hinted at a different picture: a comment about his concern for her hours, her grades, her friends. Obviously he had an active social life and a keen interest in women, or at least that was the way his daughter perceived him. Even after two failed marriages, he seemed likely to be seeking a third. This was typical for a man with a child to raise alone. Being a single parent scared most males. But the possibility of her father remarrying frightened this girl terribly.

Laura thought about Keith. He also had a daughter to raise alone and he seemed to have adjusted fairly well. He hadn't mentioned where his ex-wife lived, and he'd never talked about why their daughter stayed with him rather than her mother. That arrangement might be only temporary, for all Laura knew.

Keith's daughter had had the adjustments of divorce, which might have been pretty difficult, but this girl, Justine, had been deserted by her mother. Besides that, she had suffered the trauma of having an uncaring and difficult stepmother and a father who didn't seem to have time for her. No wonder she lacked self-identity.

"Justine," Laura began, "have you and your father discussed your arrest?"

"You keep pushing with that. I told you. The subject gets him massively hyper."

"Have you tried again to discuss it? Calmly, as I suggested. Have you told him your feelings? What was going on in your mind when you decided to shoplift, when you had plenty of money to pay for those things?"

"He wouldn't be interested."

"Did you try?"

"Not exactly."

"What do you think he'd do if you brought it up again?"

Justine didn't answer for some time. She scraped her foot over the carpet. "He wouldn't, like, hit me or anything, if that's what you're trying to find out."

It wasn't. Laura was already certain the father never physically punished Justine. What she was after was a sign of loyalty toward a parent in the midst of so much hostility. And it was here. A good sign. She decided to test it.

"Did he ever hit you?"

"No."

"Do you ever tell your father you love him?"

"No."

"Do you?"

"Do I what?"

"Do you love him?"

The girl shrugged. "I guess. He's my father, so I guess."

"Does he love you?"

"He's stuck with me."

"No he isn't, Justine. I know plenty of fathers who refuse to take care of their kids alone. They find other places for them, with relatives."

"So we don't have any relatives. So big deal."

"Nevertheless, I'm sure your dad wouldn't stay with you if he didn't want you."

"Who the hell wants a parasite?"

Laura studied her. It was clear that on one level Justine knew she was giving her father a hard time, perhaps even being unfair about fighting him so hard about his social life. But on the conscious level Justine believed she was right, and her father was wrong. Still, it was so hard to tell with this teenager what was truth and what wasn't.

"You told me you'd talked to a counselor at your old school, Justine. Did that counselor ever talk with you and your dad together?"

"What are you asking *me* for? You've seen all my records. So, like, you know all the answers."

"I've read no files whatsoever, Justine. You have no criminal record besides this one arrest. I'm required to check on court records, but not any others—not even school files—and I rarely do. I want no preconceived ideas at all. The only things I know about you are what you've told me in our talks together. What some other psychologist has concluded about you at some other point in your life is of no value to us here."

The girl stared at her with dark eyes growing softer. "What if I lie to you?"

"What do you mean?"

"If . . . you just know stuff I tell you. I could lie."

"Sure you could, but what would be the point?"

Justine shrugged.

"So I repeat my earlier question. Did you and your father ever talk to a counselor together?"

"Why?" Fear rose in Justine's eyes.

Laura understood the fear. "I wonder how willing he would be to meet with us. You don't seem to have good communication with your dad. There are several things blocking it, and we can't break through those blocks unless the two of you are willing to work together."

"Oh, man! He'd never come! No way would he ever talk about . . . like, personal stuff in front of you."

"Even if he thought it would help you?"

"Help me like how? Major farce! I don't even know what I'm supposed to be here for!"

"Of course you do. You're here because the court feels you need to work out some of your hostilities in ways other than breaking the law."

Justine twisted a lock of hair around her finger time and time again. "My dad will go totally wild. He'll have a royal cow if I ask him to come here."

"What if I ask him?"

"Well, I mean, don't. Dad's, like, turned total monster when he's pissed. And a stranger asking, like, personal stuff would tick him good."

Laura smiled softly, turning in the swivel chair toward her desk to write something. "Monster or not," she said calmly, "I think we shall ask him all the same."

The girl paled. "No, don't ask him."

"It's vital, Justine. If you can get the problems with your dad worked out and develop some communication at home, I think your hostilities will be resolved. I'm sure your dad cares how you feel about things, even if you don't believe that right now."

Her young client straightened in the chair and was staring out of the window, as she had a habit of doing when she didn't want to listen to what was being said to her.

"I'm writing down the time for an appointment," Laura said. "Next Thursday at four o'clock. If he can't make it, tell him to call me himself."

"Like, what if he doesn't?"

"I'll just have to keep trying. One way or another I'll have to convince him it's important. I think he will come, Justine. Don't worry—it won't be unpleasant. We'll just discuss some of the things that are troubling you both. Maybe you can both begin to hear how the other looks at things."

"I already know how he looks at things. It's just a massive hassle. I mean he hates to talk."

"He doesn't have to say anything. All he has to do is be here. He can listen to you if he doesn't want to talk."

Laura held out a slip of paper with the name of the mental health clinic and the requested appointment time.

THEY HAD JUST FINISHED stacking their dishes in the dishwasher when Justine reluctantly handed Keith a crumpled note.

"Miss Priss is turning rag. She's not satisfied with just me to bug. Now she wants you."

Keith looked at the paper and scowled. "She wants me there? What for?"

"What else? So you can, like, talk over all your private probs. Like having a criminal kid and like that." She thrust out her lower lip.

"I figured they'd be getting around to this, but I didn't expect quite so soon."

"I told her no way."

"Why'd you tell her that?"

"You won't go, will you? I mean, you think psychologists are geeks, total nerds, so why, like, be a hypocrite, Dad? All she'll do is go, 'Justine is totally awful and it's totally your fault.'"

"I don't think I have a choice, Tina. Your therapist can insist on it if she wants. And, anyway, there might be some benefit in it. Something may shed light on why you . . . why you seem to attract trouble like a magnet. . . ."

The girl dried her hands on the back of her jeans. "Well, I've like decided not to get in trouble anymore. I mean, it's a radical waste of major time, all this . . . It's a massive waste of your time, right? I mean, going there."

He smiled. "I'm glad to hear about your decision to stay out of trouble. Something must be going right, if you've really decided that."

"Yeah. So I have. So let's just forget it, okay?"

"What time is the appointment, Tina?"

"Why? You're not going, are you?"

"Yes. We're both going. We're going to see this thing through."

"Gross-out, Dad!"

"Look, Tina. If I'm messing up, I want to know about it. And I obviously—"

"You're doing this to punish me! I made one minor goof and I'm, like, punished forever!"

Keith sighed. He dreaded meeting with Tina's therapist more than he had dreaded anything for a long time. A conference might do some good, though he couldn't imagine what. In any case, he had to do what he could, however distasteful an ordeal it turned out to be.

He looked at his watch. "Kim is expecting us to pick her up pretty soon."

His daughter threw down the dish towel and left the room without answering. Keith, used to this behavior whenever Justine didn't get her way, ignored it and went to his room to shower, knowing it was no use trying to discuss the Thursday appointment any further. When they held opposite opinions, their wrangling went nowhere. Tina would do as he wished because she had to, but she always let him know how unfair she thought that system was.

During the past two years they had grown further and further apart. Rare were the days they sat together and talked as friends, the way they had done when she was younger, before his marriage to Nancy. His greatest mistake, it had soured everything in their lives.

He dressed in jeans and a short-sleeved cotton shirt. By the time he had returned to the living room, Tina was waiting for him. She wore new shorts and a crisp white shirt, and she was carrying her canvas overnight bag.

"Cripes! We're gonna be late by the time we pick up Kim! The movie starts, like, at seven-fifteen."

"We'll make it."

She walked in front of him through the back door to the carport. "So I guess you're going out tonight, huh?"

He had hoped she wouldn't ask. "Yeah."

"With who?"

"A friend."

"Sure! Like a woman, maybe?"

Cringing at the inflection in her voice, he answered crisply, "Yes."

"You're radically secretive about it!"

"I don't mean to be, Tina. She's someone I met at the university."

He heard her mutter a curse as he pulled around the circular driveway that led to Kim's apartment. There was no more time for questions, which was fine with him. He leaned on the horn.

Marybeth Cotter followed Kim to the car, smiling a hello to Keith. "Tina told you I'm picking the girls up after the movie?"

"Yes. I appreciate it," he said.

"We'll go out for pizza before we come home. If you're not doing anything, maybe you'd like to join us."

"I would, thanks, but I . . . ah . . . won't be home." He felt his daughter's familiar hostile glare on him before slowly driving on.

7

LAURA'S OFFICE was located in a large mental health complex—a square, single-story structure with patio gardens in the center. She preferred the shady patio for conferences when she knew her clients might be uncomfortable in conventional office surroundings. Such a conference was scheduled for Thursday afternoon with Justine Martin and her father. Justine had made it clear Mr. Martin was reluctant, even hostile, about the whole idea.

Thursday was a bright, early September day, hot, with a subtle hint in the air of changing seasons. The afternoon was breathlessly still. The kind of afternoon that reminded Laura of childhood country days of lavender blue shade, when the whole world seemed asleep, save for the lizards darting between the rocks.

Leaves of the palo verde trees trembled in the stillness; they made little whiskers of shadows in occasional sprays of sunlight that shot down through branches of a high old cottonwood. There were chairs and a table in a shady alcove.

Tina had little to say to her father as she led him through the hall and out into the patio. He, too, was silent, lost in his own thoughts, his own dread. Worse, he was aware that Laura's office was in this same building. The last thing he wanted was a chance meeting with Laura, and having to explain his presence here.

They sat on the garden chairs in brooding silence, waiting for the counselor. Small chirps of insects carried in the quiet air.

Laura, who was compulsively prompt, had been held up on the phone for an extra five minutes. She felt a strange sense of foreboding as she hurried through the wide, light green halls of the building.

She was turning a corner in the hallway, thoughts of Justine's father churning in her mind, when she nearly collided with Bernice Roark. Bernie had been coming from the other direction at an equally fast clip, carrying a notebook. Jumping back, startled, she quickly broke out in a grin. "Laura! Where have you been? I haven't seen you for days! Not even a phone call. I was coming down to your office to see if you still worked around here."

"I've been wondering the same thing about you, Bernie. I do apologize for not phoning...."

"The last I heard you had another date with your darkly handsome anthropology professor. This is getting to be a pretty regular thing, huh? You've been seeing an awful lot of him, haven't you?"

Laura felt a slight flush rise in her cheeks. "Uh...ves, I guess I have...."

"You look different. What is it about you that looks so different? Omigod, it can't be because of him that even your looks have changed, can it?"

"It could be."

Bernice clutched her hand to her chest in a mock swoon. "You mean . . . it's something real?"

"I don't know. Maybe it's make-believe. Maybe I can't even tell the difference."

"You must tell me what's been happening!"

"I can't right at this moment, Bernie; I have clients waiting and I'm already late. Stop by my office when you have time. Okay?"

"Sure. Okay."

Bernice's elated grin lifted Laura's spirits. She waved a quick salute and hurried out to the garden.

She saw Justine first, sitting at the round white table facing her. The girl looked small and nervous, but very pretty in white shorts and a pale yellow shirt. It was perhaps the first time she'd seen Justine when she wasn't slouching. Perhaps this improvement in posture was for her father's benefit.

The man was partly hidden behind the branches of an oleander bush. He sat with his back to her. But on seeing even the shadow of him, Laura's strange foreboding grew stronger. That powerful intuition that sometimes precedes a terrible or frightening happening came over her then.

Abruptly, a heavy curtain of doom fell. She was cold when there was no cold, sick to her stomach when it felt as if she had no stomach at all. Oh, God! It wasn't possible! *Keith?*

Laura's mind turned in sickening whirls. The things Justine had said came rushing back, mocking her. It didn't make sense, didn't add up. Damn it! It didn't fit with what Keith had told her about himself! Although, when she thought back now, what he had told her had been damned little. Martin. The name was the same, of course! But it was such a common name she hadn't connected it, not for a second! And he had called his daughter Tina. Tina. Justine. Laura's mouth went dry.

She stood in the shadow of the cottonwood as if frozen to the ground. She was unprepared, thoroughly unprepared, for this. And Keith would be, too, she was sure. He hadn't mentioned a word about his daughter's being in trouble. No wonder he had looked so shocked when she'd told him she worked with juvenile court. But he hadn't said anything.

In those seconds, standing there in the garden, feeling almost faint, Laura didn't want to know why he hadn't said something. Obviously, for some reason, he had preferred she didn't know. And now...what now...?

When Justine said her name, he turned around slowly. At the sight of Laura standing some twenty feet from the table, Keith seemed confused at first. Then pain of reality began to sink in.

"What's with you, Laura?" Justine asked. "Like, why're you just standing there?"

Laura barely heard the words. Her eyes were on Keith's. Confusion became shock, then shock turned to horror. He stood, staring at Laura. Then, casting a quick side glance at his daughter, he sat down again.

By this time Laura had closed the distance between them. She stood beside the table, hoping her trembling wasn't visible. She had to maintain an outward calm, for the sake of her young client.

"You're . . . Justine's father?"

Keith merely stared at her.

"I didn't know. . . ." she said in a small voice.

Keith remained silent, frowning, rubbing his fingers nervously over his chin.

Laura sat down. "I don't . . . quite understand . . . how this could be."

"What's coming down?" Tina was looking from one adult to the other, her dark eyes squinting. "Dad, what's with you, anyhow? Why are you acting so weird?" She turned to Laura. "Dad's not usually this . . . weird . . ." Her voice softened and faded when Tina looked at Laura. Confusion darkened her eyes. "Hey, what . . . ?" she asked in a high-pitched voice. "What *is* going on?"

The silence was strained and festering. Pretence would have been impossible even if it were not against Laura's strictest rules of professional conduct. Her first thought was not of Keith but of Justine. Deceiving a client who trusted her was unthinkable, yet Laura's heart screamed that Justine mustn't know.

She had to know, though; even if a lie would work, which it wouldn't. Laura's lips tightened as she looked across the table at Keith. The horror in his eyes had turned to stone. His fists were tightly clenched over the table, more noticeable because his skin was so dark against the solid white surface. His body seemed like granite, so tense as to be momentarily immobile.

The only sign of life came from Tina, who by now was sitting straight up in her chair like a cat ready to spring. Her arms suddenly shot forward, startling both adults. "Hey, damn it! Do you two know each other?"

"Yes." Laura answered so softly that she could barely be heard, still gazing at Keith as if she were in a trance. "Yes, Justine, we do. But I didn't realize you two were . . . father and daughter."

"You know each other? How could you?"

"We met quite by accident at the university."

"You mean, like, you're *friends*? Is that what she's saying? Dad?"

"We're friends, Tina," he replied quietly.

The girl's eyes flashed hostility. "Like . . . *good* friends?"

He hesitated a moment, then answered simply, "Yes."

Justine glanced wildly at Laura, then back at her father. "Massively weird, Dad! You're such good friends she didn't know you had a daughter!"

"Of course she knew. She, . . we just didn't realize she knew you."

"I didn't connect it, Justine," Laura said. "Your dad calls you Tina. The names sound so different to me. I just . . . didn't connect it."

"Yeah, well, maybe that's because he left out some major stuff about me. Like his daughter getting arrested, maybe. College profs who write fat fancy textbooks can't handle stuff like that."

Keith stared. His deep, rumbling voice seemed that of a stranger. "Damn it, Tina, I'm not ashamed of you and you know it."

"Why didn't your girlfriend know about me, then?"

The bitterness in his daughter's voice, the poison she spat with the word *girlfriend* caused him to blink. He frowned and still hadn't responded when Tina answered the question for him.

"It's yourself you're ashamed of, huh? I mean, her being a psychologist and all. So interested in, like, home environments and backgrounds and that junk. Her being a psychologist, she'd blame you, right, Dad? She'd blame you instead of me."

Laura sat in horror, knowing instinctively that Justine was right. This probably *was* the reason for Keith's secrecy. The girl might have been misdirected in her formative years, but she was extremely astute.

"Maybe..." Keith concurred. "Maybe what you say is true. I suppose it is true."

Laura jumped to his defense. "There was no reason for your dad to confide in me, Justine. Perhaps my profession had something to do with the fact that he didn't. And perhaps it had nothing to do with it. Maybe he just thought your private life was yours and none of my business."

The girl stared at her. "That's right, protect him! That's what the scene's going to be, isn't it? The two of you... all cozy..." Tears sprang to her eyes and filled her voice with a sudden, giant sob. "Dad kept you secret, too! He keeps all his rags secret from me. Well, just . . ." She jumped to her feet, the tears spilling. "Just . . . have your royal blast and all your damned secrets! Who cares? Like, *I* sure as hell don't care!"

Laura ached to comfort her, knowing how deeply she was hurt. She wanted to say, it's not what you think, but that would have been untrue. Her relationship with Keith was exactly what Justine thought! And the most devastating thing that could happen as far as this girl was concerned would be for her father to fall in love. The last time had been a disaster.

Laura reeled with confusion. Had Justine had a stepmother, or hadn't she? Was Keith the person she thought he was, or wasn't he? The one thing she'd been certain of was her client's sincerity when she'd discussed the pain of her father's second marriage and all the hurt caused by the stepmother whom her father had divorced.

Justine Martin knew her father, at least she knew certain areas of his makeup, very well. He apparently knew *her* better than one might expect. Why, then, were there so many problems between them? Hurt from a noncaring stepmother could do a lot of it. Keith's second marriage? She swallowed. Keith had told her he'd been married only once!

But Keith wouldn't lie to her! Would he? Why would he? She couldn't ask now. Not now!

Keith's pain, in his silence, was devastating. He sensed that nothing he could say was going to help matters any. His daughter had seen the truth: there was someone else in his life now and Tina, in her insecurity, wasn't able to handle it. Of course he had known she couldn't; that's why he hadn't told her. Tina was right; he'd been keeping a lot of secrets, from both her and Laura.

"You're wrong if you think we're going to gang up on you," he said finally.

"You're already ganging up on me. Like, who's the outsider around here, anyhow? Obviously, it isn't Laura!" She turned viciously. "Not Miss Priss! Man! Was I ever radically wrong about you!"

"You can't blame Laura for what she didn't know—"

"See? See what I mean? Like how you go with defending each other? Now you'll have massive garbage to talk over in the dark. Huh? Right? Wild! Like what do we do next about this damn kid? Well, don't bother getting, like . . . distracted from your you know what, because it won't do any good! I'm all through listening!"

Keith rose. "All of us are upset right now. This isn't the time to try to talk about it. We'll discuss all this at home, Tina. We'll just go home." He looked at Laura helplessly.

Tina wiped tears from her cheeks with her arm and sniffed. Not giving Laura another look, she began walking briskly ahead of him. Keith glanced back with hopelessness and hurt and embarrassment in his eyes. His forehead was wrinkled in a frown. It was a short glance; he was as eager to leave the patio garden as Justine was. Laura wondered if it was for Justine's benefit that he gave her no signal of reassurance, no gesture of goodbye. Or maybe it was because he felt no reassurance was possible.

She sat dead still and watched them walk away. Justine looked suddenly so frail and small, although physically she was neither. Certain resemblances Laura could see now—a sensitive expression about the mouth, the shape of the eyes. She hadn't seen any of those before. She hadn't seen *anything* before. A catastrophic mistake.

The silence of the garden was crushing. It closed around her like a curtain. The curtain at the end of a play. A dark symbol of the end of something.

The call of a dove sounded through the still, blue air, as if to say, you're not alone. But she was alone.

And Keith? He, too, was alone, she thought. She hadn't had any way of knowing before today how alone he really was. His doubts and fears formed a barbed barrier around him. They kept him from getting too close to his daughter. And though Laura hadn't known it, those same doubts and fears had also kept him from getting too close to her.

Her eyes misted. The blood seemed to have left her head, and only the dew of tears remained. Tears to blur the little sprays of sunlight on the grass. Tears to blur the deep green waxy leaves of a nearby lemon tree. To blur the pink and white oleander flowers that rose in profusion all around her. Tears to blur Keith's exit from the garden and from a dream they had dreamed together, when they hadn't known how soon all the colors and sparkles of a dream could change.

8

DARK CLOUDS were swinging down from the peaks of the Santa Catalinas, bringing promise of rain. Keith, sitting on the sun-warmed rocks, alone in his grief, saw the shadows move over the face of the desert. He felt the dusty earth quivering in anticipation of rain.

Rain. Vapor sucked from mountain lakes, puffed and whirled into clouds, grabbed by fickle winds, risen from earth and now returning. He lifted his face to the first cool caress of raindrops. They fell softly, playfully slapping waxy cactus leaves, pinging on boulders and thudding softly on the sand.

Breathing the fragrance of wet earth, Keith wished his own life could be as easily washed clean. But it couldn't. The agonies of past mistakes could not be washed away, now or ever. Tina had said very little on the drive back home from Laura's office building. He had heard a tiny sob from time to time. Keith had been less aware of his own silence in the car because both his mind and his stomach were churning so. The heat, with its rising humidity under gathering clouds, hadn't helped the nausea that had begun while they were still in the patio garden with Laura.

Impotent attempts to reach Tina had been futile.
Maybe, he thought, he hadn't tried hard enough. What
was there to explain to her, anyhow, about Laura? If he
admitted he was in love with her, it would only make
matters worse. Tina's worst fear was that he would fall
in love, that she would no longer be at the center of his
life, no longer feel as important to him. He admitted he
hadn't told her about his relationship with Laura because it was a threat to his already shaky relationship
with Tina.

Tina had refused to talk to him in the car, and later,
at home. During these shunned attempts to reach her,
he'd realized that it was too soon to try to talk ration-
ally. Tina was too upset. He was too upset. He hadn't
argued when she'd told him she wanted to go to Kim's;
a cooling-off period was the best solution. After taking her to the Cotters', he had driven to an isolated place
he had discovered earlier in the summer—a hiking trail
up into the foothills of the Santa Catalina mountains.

The area was deserted on this hot afternoon, with the
threat of an electrical storm tensing the air. A rattle-
snake had slithered across the path as he climbed, and
he had watched the reptile for a few moments in fascination, wondering if it was the cloudy skies that had
drawn it out from its hiding place in the shade.

His daughter's anguish was a bad enough problem
to have to tackle today, but it wasn't his only source of
pain. Regret over what Laura was thinking was eating
at him, too. He had been evasive, at the very least.
Laura would realize that her work as a psychologist

specializing in problems of teenagers kept her at bay where the subject of his daughter was concerned. He didn't want her to discover too much about him, and by now she was keenly aware of his insecurities and shortcomings. His failures. He wondered what Tina might have talked to Laura about. He knew she was given to exaggerations and lies; he'd seen this tendency in Tina all her life, and it had become worse in recent years. It was the worst of thoughts, contemplating Laura's opinion of him now.

The sound of rain all around him was a miraculous symbol of life and hope to the desert, but to Keith the rain had become a song of loneliness. In that song were memories of him and Laura, rain on their bodies. Rain in her eyes mingling there with her tears of happiness when he had said he loved her.

Lightning flashed repeatedly across the skies, getting nearer. Knowing the danger of lightning in this valley, Keith slid off the rock and into a small, natural dip in the earth, the bottom of which was sandy enough to absorb the water. It would be unwise, he knew, to hike back down the mountain while there was this much electricity in the sky. He sat huddled in the natural rock alcove he had found, letting the rain soak into his skin as he had that night with Laura. But it was not the same.

The disaster of today was his fault: the washing rain hissed this truth at him over and over. Tina believed he was ashamed of her, when in truth he had always been so proud of her. She doubted his love, when all her life she had been the sun of his world. Keith asked himself why he had always been so unable to make his feelings known.

And there was Laura. He had admitted his love for her, but he'd refused to confide in her. Keith huddled over his knees, feeling the rain on his back.

He had let them down, both of the people he loved most in the world, because he hadn't been honest with either one of them. His gut feeling told him he couldn't have them both. Like a fool he'd tried to grasp on to something that was never going to work.

He hated the disappointment in Laura's eyes and the fire in Tina's. Tina's anger and hurt he couldn't avoid; he had to try his best to work it out with her, to regain her trust, now at such a crucial time in her life. That left him with little choice. After today, Laura probably didn't want him, anyhow.

The storm passed quickly, as so often happened in the desert. When the lightning had changed from blinding streaks to mere blinking on the far horizon, Keith rose slowly from the ravine, drenched and miserable, and made his way carefully down the hiking path. Clouds blurred the usually clear view of the city below. He had come here just to try to think, not to make a decision. But a decision had been made.

HE COULD TELL the apartment was empty when he pulled into the carport; Tina had not returned from Kim's. He kicked off his wet shoes in the small utility area off the kitchen, stripped to the skin and dropped his soaked clothes into the washing machine. By the time he reached his bedroom, the phone was ringing.

He grabbed a towel. "Hello?"

"Keith, I've been trying to call you. Is everything all right? Is Justine with you?"

He blinked and sat down on the edge of his bed. "No, she's at her friend's house."

"Have the two of you had a chance to talk?"

"Not yet. She wasn't very receptive to the idea."

"I'm . . . so sorry about what happened, Keith. For Justine's sake mostly. I feel it's my fault for pushing that meeting."

"It's not your fault, Laura, it's mine. But I don't feel much like talking about it."

"We have to talk about it! There are several things we have to discuss that really shouldn't wait."

He was silent, trying to think of a way to say what he hated desperately to tell her.

"Keith? Are you there?"

"I don't know what there is . . . to talk about. . . ."

"Your daughter. I'm worried about this, Keith. She was just getting to the point of trusting me. She was doing so well. I won't be able to work with her now. Even if she'd agree, which I'm sure she wouldn't, I couldn't do it professionally because of conflict of interests. It just isn't possible, and changing therapists right at this point, for these reasons, is going to be touchy, at the very least."

He stared at the floor. "I'm powerless to do much about that, aren't I? Just as I was powerless to decide about a therapist in the first place. The court decides everything, doesn't it? I don't see what you can do, either. Tina probably isn't going to be agreeable to anything. They can make her go. Hell, *I* can make her go, but you can't force the hurt out of a kid, can you?"

Her voice was so soft that he had to strain to hear. "No, you can't force the hurt away."

He closed his eyes. "I should have been more up front with her about our . . . about you and me."

"When you feel you can, please come over here, will you, so we can talk? Not just about Tina. There's us to talk about, too, isn't there?"

Swallowing, he ran his bare foot over the rug, not knowing how to answer.

"Isn't there?"

"Laura, I'm embarrassed as hell over this whole mess."

"So am I. But it wasn't your fault. It wasn't anyone's fault."

"I'm caught in a bad place. If you and I continue . . . I don't see how I'll be able to try to reach Tina, or to straighten anything out. If it's even possible to straighten anything out."

"I know." Her voice had become very strained. "I know. But we can't just . . . not . . . Oh, damn it, what are we going to do?"

"I've thought about it, Laura. I've been thinking about it for hours. "Look, I've made an ass of myself. I've held out on you because I didn't want you to judge me."

"Who am I to judge anyone?"

"You're my daughter's therapist."

"I'm also a woman who loves you." There were tears in her voice. "You must come, Keith. Surely you value us enough to—"

"I value us enough to do almost anything, Laura— you know that."

"Enough to talk to me about what's happened?"

He owed her that, he thought. He owed her at least that one last thing. "Tonight I . . . I have to get hold of Tina. I won't urge her to come home right away if she'd rather not, but I have to try to talk to her."

"Yes. That's the most important thing right now. I'll be home all evening, so call me if you get a chance, okay? And if you can come, sometime soon . . ."

"I'll . . . try."

"Promise? You sound so hesitant."

"I promise," he said, meaning it. He'd been unfair enough to Laura already. But he knew he could do nothing but tell her in person what he had concluded in the mountains in the rain. There just wasn't any way to work things out without losing her. And there wasn't any way to salvage his pride.

IT WAS ALMOST TEN O'CLOCK when he rang her doorbell. Several minutes elapsed before she opened the door.

"Keith! I wasn't expecting you! Not tonight . . ."

He said nothing, only took her into his arms and held her while the length and depth of several minutes passed. He held her in a different way, and she sensed the sadness in him. He was changed. A stupid mistake, a quirk of fate, had turned joy into pain.

Finally she asked, "Is Justine at home?"

"No. She's spending the night with her friend. As usual."

"You talked to her?"

"I tried. Her friend lives in the same apartment complex. I went over there and took her home and we had dinner together. I couldn't smooth things over much. She's happier with her friends when she's upset, so she wanted to go back."

"Teenage girls can be good sounding boards for each other. It's lucky Justine has that outlet."

"I guess so. I sure as hell don't do her any good."

"Don't be so hard on yourself, Keith. It's never easy being the parent of a teenager."

He scowled with discomfort. "I told her I was coming here to talk to you. The evening was pretty damned strained. Tina would barely talk to me, and when she did, she cried. She feels betrayed by both of us, and jealous of you."

"I know."

"She's completely unreasonable. I don't know how much of it is real and how much is just manipulation. Or how much is just to punish me—or punish us—for being lovers."

"I'm sure it's all of the above."

"Yeah." He released her from his arms. "In any case, I didn't get to first base. I can't reach her… I don't know how to reach her. There's a mountain of debris between us."

She took his hand. "You don't look very well, Keith. Can I fix you a drink?"

"My stomach is in knots."

"I'm not surprised."

"The knots keep churning around. I've felt like hell all afternoon."

She nodded and sighed. "A little brandy, maybe?"

"I dunno. I guess so."

"I've never seen anyone so tense in my life." She motioned him into the living room, then followed. At a sideboard table, she poured two small portions of brandy, and came to sit beside him. She was barefoot, wearing shorts and an oversize pale pink shirt, the same color as the shiny nails on her fingers and toes.

"It's raining again," he said. "There's even been some flooding."

"Be very careful of flooded roads around here. The dips fill with water. It can be five or six feet deep when it looks like only inches. When you see a Dip Dangerous in Flood Season sign, don't ever take it lightly."

"Strange desert you live in." He accepted the small snifter of brandy from her. "All these storms."

"More than usual. The rivers that were dry in June are beginning to fill." She touched his arm, no longer willing to use small talk as a diversion. "I have some things I'd like to ask you, Keith."

"I was afraid you might."

"Not as a psychologist, damn it. As a friend."

He imbibed a large swallow of brandy. Laura waited, then went on. "Justine talked a great deal and with much bitterness about a stepmother. Did she have a stepmother?"

"Yes."

"And you're divorced from her?"

"Yeah. That marriage was the biggest mistake of my life."

"One of the reasons I never connected Justine with you was that you'd told me you were married only once. So naturally I assumed your ex-wife was your only wife and Tina's mother." Her eyes lowered. "You can tell me it's none of my business, Keith, but it's awfully contradicting, and—"

"I was never married to Tina's mother."

She looked up at him, her blue eyes quizzical. He would not meet her gaze.

After an awkward silence, she said softly, "Tina told me her mother left you both. Does she remember her mother?"

"She never knew her mother. We parted ways before Tina was born." Keith set down the glass, rose uneasily and walked to the window. Raindrops on the plate glass reflected the lights of the room in a million shivers of silver.

Laura uncurled her legs from under her and sat on the edge of the sofa, watching him closely.

"Tina's mother wanted to give up our child for adoption. I couldn't handle that. It was my baby, after all. My responsibility. I demanded custody and got it when Tina was two weeks old."

Thunderstruck, she gazed at his profile. Such a handsome, husky man. Sometimes she'd thought of him as not quite tamed, as if there was something wild left in him from his youth and something mysterious from the less distant past. He looked the part of a man who could be at home in an Alaskan winter or a tropical summer or a violent storm at sea. A man's man. A woman's torment. And now she saw this newly revealed dimension to him and more courage than she'd ever seen in any man. Taking on an infant child alone.... And his capacity to love...

Her eyes glazed with tears, her voice throbbed. "I wish you'd told me...."

"Tina and I don't talk about it anymore." He followed the path of a raindrop down the glass with his finger. "I made a lot of mistakes, Laura. One mistake was thinking I could keep the truth from Tina by telling her her mother was dead. I felt that would be easier for her to accept than the truth, that her mother didn't want her."

"You were right about it being easier to accept."

"But I was wrong about the lying."

"One always risks the truth coming out, and the resentment after. Is that what happened?"

"Yeah. In a temper tantrum my...her stepmother blurted it out."

Laura had gulped down her drink. She went to the cabinet to pour two more for them. "You've had your share of black cards dealt you, Keith."

Still gazing out into the night, he smiled. "The thing is, the cards aren't dealt us, Laura. We decide our own games and deal our own cards. If I've had some bad hands, it's been my own fault one way or another."

"But adopting your daughter was a victor's play, wasn't it?"

"It was. I've never regretted it for a minute, even though I've done a lousy job of being a father."

She capped the bottle and turned to face him. "How can you say that? You've been a very good father to Tina."

"Come on, Laura. You more than anyone should know—"

"Should know what? How much you love her? How many sacrifices you've made for her all her life, trying to be her mother and father both? Yes, now I know about that!"

"Things went wrong."

"Things go wrong in everybody's life. Did you think you'd be perfect?"

"I wanted to be. I didn't know how."

She approached him, pressing his shoulder gently. "You had no father yourself. How could you know what a perfect father is even *supposed* to be?"

He glanced at her. "Obviously I didn't. I still don't know."

"There's no such thing as a perfect father! There's no such thing as a perfect anything."

He smiled down at her, still not touching her. "You must be damned good at your job. If you keep this up, I'm going to feel better."

She raised both arms in a gesture of exasperation. "Oh, Keith, honestly! I'm not doing a . . . a job on you, and you know it!"

He turned toward her, his eyes soft. "I didn't mean it like that. I guess I just can't quite get over how . . . how understanding you are."

She shook her head. "I'm a woman. I see things from a woman's point of view. Women tend to view things in a gentler light than men. The love you have for your daughter is so beautiful, Keith. Don't forget, I know you both, you and Tina, and I understand things now I couldn't understand before."

"Because you're a woman?"

"Because I'm seeing the love while you keep dwelling on the mistakes. Both of you. The love is so splendid that the mistakes are minuscule in comparison."

"Mistakes with disastrous results."

"Serious, perhaps, but not disastrous."

He emitted a heavy sigh. "Serious, Laura. And today was a serious setback. I'm keenly aware of that. Tina's attitude was softening before this—I could see it. Your influence, no doubt. She was beginning to feel better about herself."

YOUR PASSPORT TO R♥MANCE

HERE'S YOUR TICKET TO ROMANCE AND A GEM OF AN OFFER!

1. Four FREE Harlequin Romances

Book a free getaway to love with your Harlequin VISA. You'll receive four exciting new romances hot off the presses. All yours, compliments of Harlequin Reader Service. You'll get all the passion, the tender moments and the intrigue of love in far-away places...FREE!

2. A Beautiful Harlequin Tote Bag...Free!

Carry away your favorite romances in your elegant canvas Tote Bag. At a spacious 13 square inches, there'll be lots of room for shopping, sewing and exercise gear, too! With a snap-top and double handles, your Tote Bag is valued at $6.99 — but it's yours free with this offer!

3. Free Magazine Subscription

You'll receive our members-only magazine, Harlequin Romance Digest, three times per year. In addition, you'll be up on all the news about your favourite writers, upcoming books and much more with Harlequin's Free monthly newsletter.

4. Free Delivery and 26¢ Off Store Prices

Join Harlequin Reader Service today and discover the convenience of Free home delivery. You'll preview four exciting new books each month — and pay only $1.99 per book. That's 26¢ less than the store price. It all adds up to one gem of an offer!

YOU'LL GET A FREE MYSTERY GIFT, TOO!

USE YOUR HARLEQUIN VISA TO VALIDATE YOUR PASSPORT TO ROMANCE — APPLY YOUR VISA TO THE POST-PAID CARD ATTACHED AND MAIL IT TODAY!

"She was doing well and I was very encouraged. I hate like the devil to have to give her up as a client. The timing of this was awful."

"Then you agree this could be a destructive situation."

"Yes. Right now Tina feels betrayed. We've both lost her trust. Maybe she feels somewhat foolish, too, because she told me—" Laura regretted the near slip of what might be best left unsaid.

He looked at her, waiting for her to continue. When she didn't, he asked, "Did she tell you I'm a private detective?"

Her eyes showed surprise.

"She's done that before. Something about being the daughter of a physical anthropologist doesn't appeal to her, I guess."

"I think it was to throw me off. To make you seem very hard to find. Or to put more mystery into your home life. It was for my benefit, I'm sure."

"And it did throw you off. I've wondered in the past several hours why you didn't somehow suspect who Tina was, with the same surname and all. But I can see now why you wouldn't."

Keith reached out to touch her hair lightly with the tips of his fingers. He gazed for some moments into her eyes. His own eyes were filled with pain, a deepening pain, which, even though anticipated, unnerved and frightened her.

He moved away from the window and went back to the sofa, knocking back a swallow of brandy as he sat down. "What's the final translation of all this, Laura? That I'm going to have to make a choice between you and Tina?"

She paled. "Oh, Keith, no!"

He gazed across at her, the pain dulling his eyes. "No? What does it mean, then?"

"It can't . . . it just can't be that cut and dried. There must be other solutions."

"I've spent the afternoon trying to think of them. I didn't come up with even one. If we keep on seeing each other, Tina will rebel worse than ever before. I know her. She's mad as hell at me for keeping you a secret, and she interprets it to mean our relationship could be lasting. Which genuinely terrifies her. She knows me too well for her own good."

"Maybe she does. If we continue to see each other secretly, she'll easily suspect it, and she'd lose even more respect for us. There is no easy answer, is there?"

"I'm beginning to think there's no answer at all. I've fallen in love with you, Laura. I've needed you for a long time without knowing I needed anyone. I've been empty without realizing how empty. Now I've found you and I realize . . ." He was no longer looking at her; he was simply staring into space.

At length his gaze shifted, almost in a startled way, and focused back on her. "Damn it, I don't know what to do!"

She sat down across from him. "Neither do I. But nothing has to be done right now, this minute. And nothing should be done before you have a chance to have a talk with her. Don't you agree?"

He nodded, but the nod seemed to be a strange kind of compromise, like putting their lives temporarily on hold before everything crashed.

"The best thing, I suppose, would be to not see each other for several days, at least."

"Yeah, that's best."

Laura's gaze lowered; she focused blankly on the carpet, feeling sorry for him, and for herself, and for Justine. Her heart was aching, and intuitive shadows warned of a deeper ache still to come. She knew he had reached the same conclusion before he came tonight, and hadn't yet found a way to say it.

His voice came softly through the silence. "I wandered around the desert and tried to figure all this out. I was so busy blaming myself that my mind wasn't functioning very logically—not that there's any logic to anything that's happened. I've been caught up in our relationship—yours and mine. I haven't been very realistic about the consequences it could have or where it could go. . . ."

"I understand that very well, Keith. After today. . ."

"Well, it was different sitting in the desert in the rain than sitting here with you tonight. I just . . . I don't . . ." His voice cracked with emotion. Echo on echo seemed to fill the still room—echoes of pain and frustration. Until at last, his voice again. "Maybe we could . . . uh . . . make a date for a week from now, have that in our minds so we can get through the few rough days coming up. Meantime, I'll try my damnedest to break through the communication barrier with Tina. I'll see if I can smooth things out with her. I'm not optimistic about reaching my daughter when she's been hurt—or thinks she's been hurt. She has several layers of hurt under this one. But I'll try. I'd like to straighten this out before she does anything crazy to get back at me."

"At us."

"Yeah."

Laura couldn't help but think how unfair it was that Keith's daughter's insecurities should cause such discord in his personal life, should in fact dictate the very core of his personal life. And Keith was letting it happen.

The consequences of his ignoring her fears and overreactions, though, were grave. Tina was at a turning point in her young life and her father knew it. Laura, as Tina's therapist, knew it. Both adults felt responsible for more than their own needs right now. And each understood the other. This was not a time for any fast moves. Slow and careful steps were called for.

"It's a good idea," she said. "Let's make the date for next week and see how the week goes. I'd like to talk to Justine, but I have the feeling she won't reciprocate. I'll have to recommend another therapist. I've been giving a lot of thought to it, but it's not going to be easy for Justine to change over now."

"You've been good for her, Laura. I wish there were a way for her to stay with you."

"So do I. But there just isn't. I have too much personal involvement now, and Tina's attitude toward me is completely changed."

He nodded and stared out the big window at the night sky.

"You look exhausted, Keith."

"I probably look better than I feel." He was used to his life being in turmoil over his daughter, but it was different this time. It was much, much harder this time.

Sensing his thoughts, Laura wanted to reach for him, to hold him against her. She wanted to be able to cry. For his sake, she wouldn't.

Too restless to sit still for long, Keith rose and went to her kitchen without a word. Moments later he returned with a glass of water and drank from it thirstily, draining the glass before he set it down. He walked to the window again, to watch the rain in motionless, blue silence.

At last he said her name as though pulling it out of some dark reach of memory within him, as though her name came from the sound of rain on glass. She heard it as it had sounded that night when they stood in the rain together, just outside that window, when he had said he loved her.

"Laura..."

She rose from the deep-cushioned chair and went to him.

"Laura..." he repeated in a stronger voice, turning toward her. "I don't want us to lose each other."

9

THEY HAD MADE A DATE for Friday, a week away, when Tina would be attending the first school dance of the year. On Thursday afternoon Keith phoned Laura at her office.

"I'm breaking our agreed upon silence," he said, "because something has come up."

At first fear gripped her. It was impossible to tell from the tone of his voice whether her fear was justified. "What's happened, Keith? Is it something about Justine?"

"No. And nothing about us. But I'm afraid I won't be able to make it tomorrow night."

"You sound upset."

"I'm upset about having to break our date. But there's been an interesting fossil find near the Mexican border, over near Bisbee, and I'm lucky enough to be one of the first specialists to be able to get to the site. I'll have to be away over the weekend."

She exhaled with relief. "You sound excited about this find."

"Yeah. It links up the prehistoric Indians in this area with the mastodons. They've found the leg bone of a mastodon with arrows embedded in it and a human skull at the same site with similar arrows. They tell me the head appears to have been severed from the body and there aren't any other human remains around there. But I'll have to examine it to come up with a theory on what it means."

"That's fascinating! It's not the first fossil proof that the prehistoric Indians in this area hunted mastodons, is it? I seem to recall something about a discovery like that."

"There was a find some years ago of mastodon bones with arrows, but those arrows were very different from these. I'll be able to tell you more after I've seen it. I'll be home Sunday night. Are you free on Monday evening?"

"Of course. We can have dinner at my house."

"Thanks. That'll give us some privacy. We'll talk then."

"Keith, how is Justine? Are things any smoother than they were?"

"Things are about the same, which translated means terrible. I tried to talk her into coming with me this weekend, but she doesn't want to miss the school dance or the slumber party afterward."

"It sounds like she's making more friends."

"Yeah. I'm not hearing the complaints about school I used to hear."

Laura was nervously doodling on a tablet at her desk, disheartened by the news that she wouldn't be seeing Keith tomorrow after all, and disappointed that he evidently had been unable to soften Tina's resentment.

"With all the storms we've had, I'll bet you'll be digging in mud instead of sand. The Bisbee area has had even more rain than Tucson this past week."

"I hadn't thought about that. Maybe I ought to take an extra pair of boots."

His voice had slowed. Now came a stiff silence.

"This has been a long week," he said finally.

"Yes, very long." Had it accomplished anything, she wondered, staying apart this week? Or was it merely a way to postpone having to deal with their problem? Keith needed time for his daughter—that much was certain. Maybe it would take a little more time. Maybe a lot more time. "My weekend will be filled with thoughts of you on your hands and knees in the mud."

"Maybe you ought to come."

"My day is completely booked tomorrow, including a court hearing. And, anyway, I have a feeling you could get so wrapped up in a crumbly old fossil you'd hardly know I was there."

"With you in my tent I might even forget why I was there."

She smiled. "Not a chance, Professor. You'll be in your natural element in a fossil field. I know you well enough by now to know how you love it. I think it'll be therapeutic to have something else to think about for a few days—something important to you, like this is."

"I'll be thinking about seeing you. That's what's kept me going this whole rotten week."

"Me too."

"Laura, I need more time with Tina. She's not showing anger now as much as she's just . . . removed from me. She's been like that for a long time, even before this, but it's worse now."

"It'll take time."

"She's balking at the counseling, but she has no choice. I'll deal with it next week, I guess."

"I'll see what I can do, too, to help with that. I'll recommend someone I have confidence in."

She heard muffled voices from his end of the line. Someone must have come in to his office.

"I'll talk to you on Monday," he said.

"Have a good trip, Keith. Remember, I love you."

He cleared his throat to let her know he was not alone. "Thanks for that. You too."

BY EIGHT-THIRTY on Monday evening, when Keith still hadn't arrived, Laura was concerned. It wasn't like him to get there so late; something had to be delaying him.

She had prepared a sour cream casserole and a fresh salad and melon balls. There were blue candles on the table, soft lamplight over a lavender linen cloth and fresh white roses from her garden in a crystal vase.

Standing at her window looking out at the Catalinas, she decided he must have been detained back at the dig. He had said he was returning Sunday—yesterday. It was very possible the scientists at the site had a bigger job there than anticipated. Maybe his Monday classes had been taught by someone else so he could stay. It had to be that. He was still at the dig, or on his way back. He could have phoned her from Bisbee. Yet maybe he couldn't. Bisbee was likely a distance on very rough desert roads from where Keith was camping.

By ten o'clock she knew for certain he wasn't coming. Her darkest fears loomed coldly over conscious thought: Keith had been removed enough from their situation to have made decisions on his own about it. He'd decided the kindest thing to do was to break quickly and without the agonies of goodbye. Just...break it here, with the memories to keep and no more gathering of pain....

"No!" she cried aloud, jumping up from the white sofa, spilling white wine from a long-stemmed glass. No! Keith wouldn't do that! He wouldn't! If he wasn't here, there was a reason. The reason was either his work or his daughter, and later he would explain how unavoidable it was. Absolutely unavoidable.

Although in her head she knew he wasn't going to come, her heart didn't give up until nearly midnight. It was an overcast evening, with low-hanging clouds holding the day's heat down close to the earth—an unusually warm evening for September.

Laura opened the doors and windows of the large room to invite the late-night breezes. It was dense black outside with the clouds covering the moon. A muggy gloom seemed to fill the world on this once eagerly anticipated night with the man she loved more each passing day. Keith's night, and hers, and he wasn't here!

She couldn't very well phone his home. If Tina was there alone, she'd be asleep. If Keith was there, he'd surely have called. Tina wouldn't exactly welcome her inquiries, especially in the middle of the night. Laura slowly closed the sliding glass doors, replacing the black gloom of the night with the gray and lavender shadows skulking on high white walls.

Numbly she undressed and got into bed, and lay staring into darkness for a long time. Fear gave way to heartsick thoughts that Keith wasn't within her reach, not tonight, as she lay in the bed where he had made love to her. Not tomorrow, when surely she would know why he hadn't come as promised. And perhaps not ever, because he couldn't find the place to fit her in his life.

Crying might help, she thought, but she wouldn't cry. Stubbornly she fought the negative images that pressed through the still, blackened room. Keith didn't get back from the desert on schedule. What was there to get so distraught about? Tomorrow he'd explain. Tomorrow, when she saw him.

AN EARLY MORNING call to the university confirmed what she was certain of already: Keith wasn't in, and he hadn't been there yesterday. The secretary who took the call insisted she had no idea whether he was still at the fossil dig site, and suggested Laura call back later when someone might be there who knew.

She phoned Canyon del Oro High School to find out if Justine was in attendance this morning. She wasn't. Becoming more concerned with each passing moment,

Laura dialed Keith's apartment. The wait lasted for only one ring.

"Justine? I'm just checking to see if everything is all right."

There was a long pause from the other end, so long that Laura feared the girl might hang up on her. Then a cool, "Like, why wouldn't it be?"

It was a time for careful choice of words, in order to avoid being cut off with the click of a receiver. "Your school reported you absent yesterday and today both..."

"That's because I don't feel good." The girl's voice was cold and shaky. She did sound sick.

"What's the matter?"

"It's like a stomach flu or something. Dad's got the same thing."

This Laura hadn't expected. Surely he wasn't too sick to make a hurried phone call.... "Is your dad there?"

"Yeah, but he's asleep. He can't go to work today."

"Have you called a doctor?"

"No, we'll be okay."

"Justine, are you sure your father can't come to the phone?"

"Hey, I got my orders in English, okay? He doesn't want to be disturbed by anybody."

"Isn't... isn't there something I can do? Do you need anything?"

"Yeah! To be left alone. Like, final. Dad isn't into seeing you anymore. Everything's down. I don't have to see you anymore, either."

"That's right, you don't. But I'd still like to talk to you, Justine. Would you agree to talk to me?"

"Like, what's to talk about? What could you dig out of me that you don't already know?"

"I don't want to know anything. It would be nice if we could talk as friends."

"We're not friends!"

"I had begun to think of us as friends. Has my acquaintance with your father completely destroyed all that?"

"Yes. You knew it all the time, and lied to me!"

"If I had, Justine, do you think I'd have been silly enough to set up that meeting as I did?"

Silence. Then, "So who knows what shrinks'll do? I don't want to be friends."

"All right. I respect your choice in that. But you don't sound very well. . . . Are you—"

"Look, everything's cool, okay? We caught, like, stomach flu or some crud, that's all. So we're home. And you can tell my school that, if they're so bugged about where the hell I am."

"I think you'd better call and tell them yourself, or have your dad call. You don't want this to go down as truancy."

"Oh, big whoop! What'll they do, like throw me in jail?"

Justine's voice and manner concerned Laura. She detected a kind of panic in her hostility. Laura's senses had shifted to full alert. Suspicion hounded her. Something was wrong.

Laura's thoughts whirled, soared and dived like a seabird above opaque water—searching for something that wasn't even there to find. What *was* going on? She was convinced the girl was trying to hide something. And from the fright in her voice, it could be something serious.

If that strange telephone conversation had been with any other client, Laura's first impulse after hanging up the phone would have been to notify juvenile authorities that there should be a check on her supervision.

Instead, she got up from her kitchen table, splashed the remains of her coffee hurriedly into the sink and picked up her handbag from the counter. She'd never been to Keith's apartment, never seen where he lived. Come to think of it, she'd never been invited. She wasn't invited now, either. But she had a responsibility where Justine was concerned. Something was wrong over there, and welcome or not, she was going to find out what it was.

Driving the long, twisting streets toward the valley center, Laura was no longer merely theorizing that there was something portentous about Justine's conversation. She was absolutely certain of it. Her insides were twisting with anxiety.

Mingled frustration and impatience made it harder for her to find the Martins' apartment in the complex. It was a pleasant, uncluttered atmosphere, she observed. Desert gardens surrounding low, tile-roofed structures with a Spanish motif. Driveways shaded by mesquite bushes and palo verde trees. Adobe brick patio fences.

She pulled into the driveway, noting with a flush of fear that Keith's car wasn't in the carport, probable evidence that Tina had lied to her about his being home in bed with stomach flu. The place was so quiet on this warm Tuesday morning that the crunching sound of her footsteps on the gravel walk sounded unnaturally loud. Guided by curiosity and dread, she rang the front doorbell twice before Justine opened the door.

The surprise showed in her pretty face. Strangely, not anger, only surprise. "Laura?"

"It was either me or your probation officer, Justine. In fact, he could be right behind me, although I hope not. I'm surprised he hasn't already been notified of your absence by the school. That's part of what being on probation is all about."

Dressed in jeans and a T-shirt that must have been Keith's, and, for a change, no makeup, Justine stood in the doorway looking stunned. "Why did you come? I told you Dad was . . ."

"You told me he was ill. I don't think he is. I don't think he's even home, is he?"

The shock on the girl's face changed swiftly to anger. "So it's not me you're worrying about, is it? It's him!"

Laura kept her voice soft and steady in spite of her growing certainty that Justine was hiding something. "I'm worried about both of you."

"What are you worried about me for? Like, I look dead or something? Like, the sight of me is worth a trip?"

"You don't look like someone who's been sick for two days."

"Okay, so I ditched school. What are you going to do about it?"

"I'm not going to do anything about it. I'm not your counselor anymore."

"Oh, whoop! You're only just my father's rag of a girlfriend. And that's like a license to go checking up on me!" She turned away. "Well, just . . . go away, okay?"

Laura studied her in the shade of the doorway. She'd never seen Justine like this. She was like a half-lit fuse looking for any excuse to explode. And it wasn't anger. The anger was only a cover-up; Justine was very frightened.

Gently Laura reached out and touched a slender shoulder. "Why did you tell me he was here?"

The girl turned toward her once again and stared, stress lines forming about her eyes. She seemed to be digesting Laura's question slowly, very very slowly, as though she had been hypnotized and was just coming awake.

"Justine? Where is he?"

Tears formed in the girl's blank, dark eyes. She blinked once, and looked away, then back again.

With constricting throat, Laura moved closer. "Justine?"

"I don't know!" she blurted. "I don't know where he is!"

Laura blanched with alarm. The girl's stare touched off cold tremors within her. Intuitively she knew that this, finally, was the truth. She fought for control under a storm of anguish that gathered force with each passing second. Laura nearly reeled as she began to assimilate the implications of such a frighteningly unexpected revelation.

In a thin, unsteady voice, she asked, "He hasn't come home from his weekend trip?"

"For sure you'd know all about that." Justine's words remained harsh, but her voice quavered and her eyes were filled with tears.

"I talked to him on the phone on Thursday. He said he was going out of town. When did you expect him back?"

Tina wiped her cheeks with her arm. "Sunday."

Laura had somehow suspected Keith wasn't home with Justine today, but she hadn't been prepared for a jolt like this. He hadn't returned from the dig at all!

She reached for Justine's hand. "You've been here alone, and worrying ever since Sunday? Why on earth didn't you let someone know, Justine? Why did you try to keep it from me when I called this morning? Did you try phoning the university yesterday?"

The girl sniffed. "I didn't get, like, really worried till last night.... I know Dad when he's grossly involved in work. I was ... like, you know, there's no phone out there."

"That's true. He's probably on his way back. He must have been held up."

"He'd have called by now!"

He would have, Laura thought with a sinking heart. Yes, he would have.

Justine managed to look her in the eye for the first time that day. "After you phoned me this morning I did call the university and they told me...they told me..." A sob trembled to the surface.

Weakness crept through Laura's legs. "What did they tell you?"

"He left the dig Sunday morning, like, eleven o'clock. They don't know where he is...."

Laura's eyes closed. She felt dizzy all over again, but she was determined not to show her fear to Tina.

The girl's face constricted with pain. Another great sob made her shoulders shake. "I'm scared...."

If only, Laura thought, she'd known yesterday that Keith hadn't returned on schedule. If only they hadn't made that stupid agreement not to communicate until Monday night. If only she'd gone with him as he'd playfully suggested. If only...if only...

When she put her arm around Tina's shoulder, there was no pulling away this time. She could sense the girl's relief, however reluctantly it had come, in not carrying this burden of fear all alone.

"I'm scared..." she repeated.

"Did they tell you anything else, anything at all?"

"They didn't know until this morning that he...I mean, like, the people there thought he was here and the people here thought he was there, or something. I don't know. They go, 'We've just...we've just...'" The sobs came harder.

"Just what? What, Justine?"

"They just had called the . . . the state p-police about it. . . . The *police*, Laura!"

Laura swallowed a lump that wouldn't leave her throat. She couldn't believe anyone could have been so insensitive as to frighten Keith's daughter this way. "Did the person you talked to at the university know who you were?"

"No. I said I was a friend of his. People never tell kids anything."

"You knew this when I came and you weren't going to say anything?"

"Like, maybe I thought it's got nothing to do with you."

"Do you still feel that way?"

"I don't know," she said, crying. "I'm just... scared. . . ."

"I think the most likely explanation is that he had car trouble."

Tina sniffed. "He has a lot of trouble with that damned car. . . ."

"That's probably it," Laura said, not believing it herself. If the information Tina got was correct, it had been nearly forty-eight hours since anyone had heard from Keith. Too many hours missing to attribute to car trouble. Still, he was in an isolated area. It was possible. "They'll begin a search. They'll find him if his car is stalled somewhere."

The fierce resentment Laura had sensed from Justine earlier on the phone had given way to a greater, more pressing need. And loneliness. And fear. Laura's heart went out to her. She'd been all alone when she'd heard her dad was officially missing, just before Laura's arrival at her doorstep, and the terror had been building ever since.

Laura led her to the couch and urged her gently to sit down. "Until they do find him, we have to come up with a place for you to stay. You can't stay here alone."

"Why not? I live here."

"It wouldn't be wise, and besides your well-being is of general concern to—"

"Yeah, I know. Like, I'm the geek on probation."

"I'll have to see about finding you somewhere to stay, unless you can stay with friends. Do you think that's possible?"

A spark of anger flashed through the tears in her eyes. "What do you care where I stay?"

"Look, I'm going to level with you. Evidently word of your dad's . . . delay is just out. I'm guessing that at any moment there's going to be somebody over here to . . . take over responsibility for your well-being until Keith gets back, even if it's for just a few hours. I think you'd be a lot happier with any arrangements we can figure out now, before strangers get into the act. Damn it, Justine, I can help you. So let me!"

She sniffed again and blinked. "Kim Cotter's mother wouldn't mind if I stayed there. I'm at their house half the time, anyhow."

"I'd like to ask her, though, to make sure it's all right. Okay?"

Tina blinked and nodded.

What all this meant hadn't been absorbed yet by either of them, Laura knew. Anything they could do before the horror really sank in would make it that much easier for Justine during the coming hours until Keith . . . until he returned.

"Don't you think we ought to forget our differences for a little while, Justine? That is, if we have any differences?"

Tina grabbed her arm. "They won't make me stay in some institution, will they?"

"No, I'll see to it you can stay with friends."

"Will they listen to you?"

"Yes."

"What if he's like hurt or something? What if—"

Laura stopped her with a gentle squeeze of the hand. "Don't play what if. There could be a thousand what ifs."

"It's one of those what ifs, though, right? Dad's absolutely missing!"

"The explanation might be a very simple one."

Tina covered her face and sobbed into her hands as each passing second sharpened and brightened the fear. "If he could . . . he'd call me . . ."

"That's true, he would. But there are no phones in the desert. Your dad is used to being in wild country. If he's stranded by car trouble, I'm sure he'll be all right." She squeezed Tina's shoulder assuredly. "Where can we find Mrs. Cotter?"

"She works at Globe Travel Agency."

"On Oracle? Good, that's very close. Now, what do you think about going to school? It seems to me the worst thing you could do is sit home alone like this and worry."

"Will they make me go to school?"

"I don't know. But your friends are there, aren't they?"

Tina nodded.

"Why not let me take you to school, then? I'll tell the office why you're late and make sure you'll be told as soon as your dad is contacted or gets back. Okay?"

"You're trying to get me out of here. You think somebody is going to come here."

"Yes. You can wait if you want to, of course. The choice is yours."

"I want them to leave me alone!"

Laura sat quietly, doing her best to stay outwardly calm, for Justine's sake. Finally she said in a soft voice, "That may not be one of your choices, but if you want to stay..." She rose slowly.

"Dad could walk in any minute!"

"Yes. But as you said, when he gets near a phone, he'll call before he comes on in to Tucson, knowing you'll be worried." She paused, studying Tina's frightened eyes.

"The wait may be less than an hour, for all we know. I'm just trying to keep things from getting any more difficult for you in case it's longer. I'm here for you, Justine, if you want me to be. I'm not officially your counselor, though; I'm not going to force myself on you."

The girl sighed shakily. "I'm a massive mess. I need to get dressed...."

"Go on and get ready for school, then. I'll wait."

Driving to her office after she had left the high school, Laura gripped the steering wheel tightly, fighting back the tears of fear that threatened to blur her vision of oncoming traffic. Her shoulders were stiff with tension. It had been such a struggle to appear confident that Keith was all right. She wasn't confident of it at all. Forty-eight hours in the desert was a long time, especially in this late-summer heat.

At least it wasn't the dry season. There had been so much rain. Pulling up into her parking space at the mental health clinic, she thought about the rain. The Bisbee area had had tremendous rains over the weekend, added to already full rivers and heavy mountain runoffs. News reports had described flooding. Some roads had been flooded out. That was it! Keith had to detour to avoid flash floods and got lost.

That wasn't likely. But the flooded roads were a fact. A search party would examine the flooded areas, of course. Laura tried to force herself to think positively. Her mind wouldn't let her do otherwise, even with the weak knees and the ache in her neck. Already two hours late, she sat in her car for several minutes, trying to calm herself enough to face the working day. With her arms across the top of the steering wheel, Laura lowered her head, no longer able to hold back tears. "Keith..." she said aloud. "Oh, God, what's happened? Keith ... where *are* you?"

10

THE HOURS OF THAT DAY were agonizingly slow, and the next day was worse. A man couldn't just disappear, yet the searchers found no sign of him. Laura telephoned Mrs. Cotter on that second bleak, endless evening to see how Justine was holding up under the strain. She was doing as well as could be expected and had gone to school that morning.

Laura ate very little and slept only restlessly. It was the sort of waiting on which every passing hour built more fear. The longer Keith was missing, the more likely it was that something serious had happened to him.

On Thursday morning Keith's car, or what was left of it, was found by sheriff's deputies in Cochise County, more than a hundred miles from the fossil discovery. The car had been washed down a raging, flooding river. All its windows were smashed.

Laura made an inquiry of her own. There had been flash floods for miles around, the sheriff told her; the car could have been caught in any one of them. Anyone inside had a poor chance of surviving. Laura could sense that now the search for a survivor would be less intense; the deputies didn't think Keith was alive.

It was like a terrible dream that was not a dream. She felt paralyzed by the utter helplessness that grabbed and wouldn't let go of her. Keith was alive. He had to be. Nothing in her mind or in her heart would allow her to believe otherwise.

Knowing that the discovery of his car would be in evening news reports, Laura canceled her afternoon appointments and drove to the high school. She waited until classes were over to avoid frightening Justine too much, and found her in a group of students, waiting for the bus.

It wasn't easy, while they walked across campus, having to tell her about the car, but it was better for her to learn of it this way.

"What we know for sure now is that your dad couldn't get back because of the floods. No foul play or anything, Justine—it was the floods. He isn't used to southern Arizona and ground that can't absorb rainwater and roads that wash out."

Tina seemed unable to look at her. She stared at the ground as if she were afraid to raise her head. "They think he drowned, don't they?"

Laura knew the girl was fighting back tears. "I don't know what they think. I know what I think, though. Your dad told me about his treks in Kenya. He's no stranger to the elements. He's used to wilderness areas and he's an unusually strong man and an excellent swimmer. I don't believe for one minute that he drowned. He lost his car, and he's on foot. It's pretty vast country, but they'll find him. I know they will."

The girl's chest was heaving. "Oh, I want to believe you!" She turned, finally to meet the woman's eyes. "He has to be alive, Laura! He has to be!"

"Yes," she agreed softly. "He has to be."

Laura drove Tina home so she could check the mail and pick up a few things before she went to Kim's. With the air conditioning off, the apartment was stuffy and hot. Tina went at once to the refrigerator and took out a cola.

"Do you want one?"

Laura opened the patio door to let in a small breeze. "I sure do. I don't think the heat will ever let up this year."

There had been a change in Justine since Keith's disappearance. The fear of losing her father was pushing out the other resentments. Justine was being forced to think about what it would be like without him, with the inevitable result that she was appreciating him in a new way. Now that she could not take for granted that he would always be there, the thought of his not being there had sobered her, was terrifying her. She no longer had the energy or the incentive to fight Laura.

The strain in the relationship—Laura and Justine's—was a wavering thing, present one moment, forgotten the next. Today Keith's car occupied their minds too much to allow a great many other thoughts in, yet they discussed it very little.

"I miss him," the girl said as she stood beside Laura in the patio doorway with the can of cola. "I never thought I could miss him this much."

I miss him, too, Laura thought. *Oh, how I miss him!* She closed her eyes, feeling the warm breeze on her face.

"Dad and I didn't get along all that massively great the past couple of years; like, we were mad at each other a lot."

Laura was watching a hummingbird dart about the eaves of the patio porch. "Don't forget, Justine, that your dad was an orphan. He didn't have a father to model for him what fathers are supposed to be, and he had no way of knowing. All he knew was that he loved you. The only guide he's had was that love. Sometimes he made mistakes, but I don't think he made any more than any other parent. He's made far less than many."

"Sometimes I forget," the girl said in a tiny voice, "that he was an orphan and I . . . I wasn't."

Laura smiled softly. "Nothing is ever all bad, Justine. Maybe things will be better between you when he gets home. Fear of losing someone makes one appreciate that person more."

"He will get home, right, Laura?"

"I'm not ready to give up believing that. Are you?"

"No. He has to, that's all! They're still looking for him, aren't they?"

"Of course. And they'll find him. Or he'll find them, one way or the other."

She couldn't admit her concern that they weren't searching hard enough or well enough. With several roads washed out, Keith might have been driving in a place they wouldn't have expected. She wondered how long the intensive search would last. Were they already pulling back on manpower? Yes, damn it! Since the discovery of that car, she knew they were.

Laura took Justine back to the Cotters' apartment and drove straight home, so restless and frustrated that she felt she might explode. The feeling of helplessness was driving her crazy.

In her study she began digging for her maps of southern Arizona. Wine helped steady her nerves; she'd finished two glasses before she placed the telephone call to Bernice.

THE TWO OF THEM were bent over the maps in Laura's kitchen as the afternoon became evening, and the skies changed from bright blue to pale pink.

"There are limited ways Keith could have come north from the border area," Laura pointed out. "The university situates the dig site right here, and there was heavy flooding through this area directly north, all up and down the San Pedro. The car was found here...."

"That's a long way away from the dig, Laura." Bernice frowned, scratching her head.

"The car was in water that came down from the San Pedro River and also from the Pico. Water from a lot of flood runoffs found its way to those rivers, so the location of the car isn't very helpful." Laura slid a polished nail along the map. "I remember from when I was a kid how the streams down the south side of the mountains here would overflow during the flood season and wash out the roads down below. It happened almost every year. In as bad a flooding as there was last weekend, any of the arroyos that filled in this area could have washed a car downstream."

"In other words, you're saying the car could have been on one of *these* roads when the flood water took it."

"I'm sure it was, Bernie, because Keith was driving northeast from Naco. If he detoured because of floods along the San Pedro, he'd have come up this way, run into flash flood warnings around Sierra Vista, where the flooding was really bad, and come around this way."

Bernice frowned. "You may know this area very well, Laura, but he doesn't. There are a lot of small roads along here, none of them very good."

"I've spent hours going over this. If Keith is alive, I think he's in this area—" she made a small circle on the map "—and he's stranded, so he'll have searched for some kind of shelter from this damned heat wave. He wouldn't try to venture far into the desert. Or he could be . . ."

"He could be hurt."

"Yes."

"Or he could have drowned, or . . ."

"I know all that, Bernie. But Keith is very strong and I refuse to believe he isn't . . . all right."

Bernice sighed. "Love doesn't have to be logical, does it; it only has to be based on faith, so what can I say? I've been dreading to ask this for the past half hour, so why put it off any longer? You want to use my pickup, right?"

"Yes."

"Laura, if the searchers with their helicopters can't find a man, I don't see how you can expect to do any better."

"I know the area better, especially if he's right in here where I suspect he might be. When I was a kid I rode my pony over every mile of this land. I know every road and every stream. There are some specific places I'd like to look."

"Of course you can use the pickup, Laura. But I'm sorry, I just can't share your optimism. It's been four days now, five tomorrow. Surely if Keith was all right he'd have found some way back by now. But then, what do I know? When do we start and what do we need?"

Laura smiled at her over the maps. "Was that a we I heard?"

"I can't let you go out there alone."

"I've spent a lot of my life out there alone."

"This is different. You might need some help. Though, mind you, I don't share your conviction that you can find him."

"You ought to have more faith in me. I know he could very likely be in that area, and if he is there, we'll find him. I know where to look."

"It sounds like a real long shot. Besides which, you could be setting yourself up for an awful disappointment."

"I realize the risks. But I'm going insane around here—just this horrible, helpless waiting. I can't stand it anymore. I have to do something!"

"You don't trust the search parties?"

"They were doing a great job before they found that car. I don't think they're looking for a survivor now. They may be giving up, but I'm not going to."

"We'll need supplies. I'll help you if you'll give me a list."

"You're a good friend, Bern. The best."

"I just hope you know what you're doing." Bernice looked at her watch. "I'll go to the store and fill up the gas tank. Then I'll stop by home and get what I need and stay over here tonight. You'll probably want to be rolling out of here before sunrise."

"I'm so impatient I wish we could leave right now."

"Morning will have to be soon enough. We can't get out of here before then. What could we accomplish at night, anyhow?"

Laura straightened and touched her friend's arm. "How can I ever thank you enough?"

"There's nothing to thank me for. Let's just hope that sweet little Toyota truck of mine can do what the helicopters couldn't!"

RAIN HAD CONTINUED in most of Santa Cruz and Cochise Counties through the past weekend and into the week. By Tuesday night the skies had begun to clear, and there hadn't been any rain since then. Evidence of the flooding was everywhere—washed-out portions of road, debris left by rushing water. But the desert reclaimed its identity very quickly; most of the rocky soil already looked dry again.

Laura had drawn up a careful list of places a person might find shelter and water. There weren't many such places, for streams and springs were not plentiful here. Some tree-shaded areas, deserted farms. The first day they found nothing, but Laura would not be discouraged. Because of the conditions of the roads, travel was slow.

In Patagonia they stopped to use the phone. Still no news in Tucson about Keith. He seemed to have disappeared from the face of the earth.

Laura said, "We should be able to reach a cutoff road that leads to Ocotillo Springs before it gets too dark. The road is hardly better than a cow trail, and I'm not optimistic about how much road is still there."

"Ocotillo Springs? What's that? It can't be a town if there's only a cow trail to it."

"It used to be a town. Until the nearby copper mine closed in about 1907. All that's left are walls of a few buildings and the old general store, which is pretty well preserved."

"A ghost town? I love ghost towns!"

"I used to like to prowl around that old store when I was a kid. Wallpaper was still on the walls, and the counter was still there. I think the stable across the street will still be intact except for the roof, and a couple of the stores nearby are probably still standing. There's a natural spring, so some very large cottonwood trees thrive there."

Bernice was scowling; the road on which they were traveling was very rocky, and this was the "good" road.

"So you think Keith might be holed up in a ghost town?"

"If he's stranded somewhere, it wouldn't be in open desert."

"Goose chase," Bernice insisted.

"No, it isn't. A runoff from the Pico would form arroyos along here, which is about the only route across this lower section. The sheriff told me the water was over eight feet deep and moving like hell down Cottontree Canyon. It caught two cars."

"I heard. The occupants in both cars were drowned."

"But that was Sunday morning, Bernie. Keith would have had to go around it by Sunday afternoon. I just know he went around. And this is the only way around unless he doubled back."

Chewing on a long piece of red licorice, Bernice muttered, "What I'd like to know is, why isn't the search party smart enough to figure all this out? They're supposed to be the experts."

"They wasted too much time along the San Pedro. They did look in this area, and rather well, but they were using helicopters. Nobody's been out here on foot." Laura's eyes misted. "He has to be somewhere, damn it. As long as they haven't found a . . . a body, he must be alive."

"Not necessarily. Not with all the wild animals in this area."

She pounded her fists together. "You didn't have to say that!"

"No, I didn't. But one of us has to keep a hold on reality, Laura. You've got to prepare yourself for anything, whether you want to or not." Bernice's hand folded over hers. "Look, it's getting dark and we can't take on any of these trails at night. Start looking for a place to pull over. We'll have something to eat and get a little sleep. Okay?"

Laura nodded and smiled. "Okay. We'll open the bottle of Southern Comfort and toast tomorrow's sunrise."

THE SUN WAS HIGH by eight o'clock. Tall grasses at the edge of the road swayed lazily in the midmorning breeze. The rocky, ragged road under them was hardly passable and getting worse.

As the vehicle lurched to the side, Bernice emitted a string of curses. "There's no damned road left, Laura! We can't make it up here without four-wheel drive. We'll have to walk in."

"Okay. Those trees look less than a mile away. That's not too bad a hike." She reached around for the canteen of water.

"This is something of a long shot," Bernice said softly, taking Laura's hand. "I can't bear to see you disappointed if this—"

Laura interrupted. "Maybe it is a long shot, Bernie, but turn around and look at that road down there, where we were last night. The mountain runoffs washed over it in a dozen places—real flash floods. If Keith's car had been caught in any one of them, it could have ended up in the river flood. And a man stranded along this route would need shelter, wouldn't he?"

"Yeah, it's a convincing theory, I'll admit. It's just scary because this country is so damned big!"

"It isn't when you know it. If Keith went another of half a dozen ways, we're chasing a cold trail. The sheriff thinks he went straight north, but I don't. There's a very good chance he came this way, especially if Cottonwood Canyon was under water. Come on, Bernie, we're wasting precious time."

"Yeah, we are. Let's go, then. Watch out for rattlesnakes."

It was an uphill climb to reach Ocotillo Springs. Luckily the day was young, its sun not yet hot. The big dark trees became bigger and darker as they neared their destination, and as the silence of the desert closed in around her, Laura became more frightened with each step. *You don't win games like this,* her heart scolded in the lonely, haunting song of a desert bird. She'd been a fool to try. It was wishful thinking because she couldn't bear to lose him. Now she could no longer see the sunshine of the blue September day. Everything had gone all black and cloudy. The very air had begun to tremble.

After a rough hike through dense desert growth, they stood in the shadows of those massive trees, looking down the main street of a town long dead. Except for one small puddle, there was no sign of the week of heavy rain. Only dust here now, raised by their footsteps as they moved. The air was filled with the heaviest silence Laura had ever heard.

The town was exactly as she remembered it. One structure stood above the others, its wooden siding long bare of paint, save for faded lettering above the door: General Store. There was no door on the front, no glass or frames left in the windows. An old shutter swung limply, catching on the passing breeze, squeaking mournfully. The sagging hitching post in front of the store was still there. "There's nothing here, Laura," Bernice whispered, as if afraid to have her voice crack the heavy silence.

Eyes searching the ghostly street, Laura experienced an ominous, unfamiliar feeling deep within her. A premonition.

Bernice's hand clutched at Laura's arm. "If we see one buzzard, I'm bolting!"

Laura scowled. "Will you stop that? Come on, let's look around."

"For what? Omigod! There is a buzzard! Over there!"

"That's a crow! What's the matter with you, Bernie?"

"I hate this place! It feels so strange."

"Yes, it does. Very strange."

"Is that why we're whispering?"

"I guess so." The strangeness, Laura thought, could be the sensation of something dying inside her. She had been so hopeful, figured so carefully. This was one of the last places on her list. And they'd found only silence and the ghosts of a past that had nothing to do with them.

They began walking in slowly, as though they didn't know what else to do. Suddenly, Laura blinked sunlight from her eyes and her breathing jerked to a stop. Her heart lurched wildly. A figure was darkening the doorway of the store—the figure of a tall, huskily built man, but bent, leaning heavily against the side of the door, shading his eyes to the desert sun!

Not trusting her own eyes, she blinked, then blinked again. Her voice was inaudible as she mouthed his name.

Slowly sensation pumped down from her heart into her numb legs; slowly life came back. "Keith!"

Then she was running down the weed-grown street, her boots throwing up dust, her heart pounding so wildly that she thought it would burst.

He didn't move or straighten his sagging body in the frame of the doorway. Nor did he reach for her. By the time she was near enough to see his face, behind the growth of several days' beard, his body was hunched even more.

His eyes, duller than she'd ever seen them, were glazed with utter astonishment. "Laura?"

He slid down the side of the doorway as though he were no longer able to stand. "Laura . . . I don't believe it. . . ."

His voice was so soft and weak that she barely recognized it.

He mumbled again, almost deliriously, "I just don't believe it...."

Weakly his arms reached out to her as she knelt in the doorway beside him, tears in her eyes, on her cheeks. Words wouldn't come. Only the feel of his body, warm and alive, mattered. The pounding of his heart, the exhaling of his breath, warmth of his skin. He was alive!

They held each other in the heights and depths of the sweetest joy Laura had ever known until he whispered, "Am I hallucinating? Am I dying and only imagining ... you here?"

"I'm here. Can't you feel me?"

"Yes..." He closed his eyes.

She pulled slightly away, and studied him. Skin very pale under the beard. Heavy lines of stress and exhaustion around his closed eyes. Dust in his thick hair. Perspiration soaking his torn shirt. She remembered he had been barely able to stand.

"You're hurt! How badly are you hurt?"

"Not that bad—just my ankle, but it's too damned painful to walk on." He grimaced, trying to move the foot. "Is Tina all right?"

"She's frightened. Your car was found washed down the river. We've all been scared to death."

"So have I. I was just about to give up hope of anybody finding me out here." For the first time he noticed Bernice, who had decided their private reunion had gone on long enough. She approached and stood over them.

"Scared is hardly the word." Bernice smiled. "Laura has been a person possessed. She was determined to find you."

Wiping tears of joy from her cheeks, Laura couldn't take her eyes from his. "You said we couldn't lose each other, Keith! I knew you wouldn't leave me."

Bernice knelt beside them with more immediate and practical matters on her mind. "When did you have food or water last?"

"Food, I don't know. But water was no problem. The roof leaked puddles on the floor, and there's a small stream by the trees I could drag myself to . . ."

Laura tried to smile as she brushed his dusty hair from his eyes. "I warned you about our desert floods. I'll bet your car stalled in an arroyo. Let me see your foot."

He was wearing only one boot. The ankle was badly swollen.

"I've never seen water rush down so fast in my life. . ." he said, and winced when Laura touched the injured ankle.

"Is it broken?"

"I don't know. I think it must be."

"We have food in the camper. Oh, why didn't we bring any with us, Bernice? Oh, Keith! We're parked a mile away. You'll never make it that far!"

"Don't panic, Laura. Somehow I'll make it."

He grunted as he tried to rise. Laura reached an arm around him. "How will you make it? You can barely stand up."

One on each side, the women tried to help him over the uneven, splintering boards of the porch. But even a few steps seemed too much for him. His already damp shirt was soaked in less than a minute. With a groan, he sagged to his knees.

"I don't know which is worse," he moaned. "The weakness or the pain.... The pain, I think...."

"Damn, I wish we had four-wheel drive so we could get in here," Bernice complained. "I don't know what we're going to do ..."

"We need a helicopter!" Laura said suddenly.

"Sure. Seen any around we could thumb a ride from?"

"There are several around here, Bernie! Some of the big ranches keep them. We passed the Harvey place on the way up here this morning. They have a helicopter there!"

"They do? You're sure?"

"Of course I'm sure!"

"Wow! Private helicopters! And I thought cowboys still rode the range on pintos. I'll go!" She touched Keith's shoulder. "Just hang in there, Keith. I'm fast as hell when I want to be."

Her feet pounded against the ground as she sprinted down the street of the ghost town and disappeared into the thick of desert growth.

Sitting in the dust, Keith wiped perspiration from his forehead.

"I never saw anyone disappear so fast in my life," Laura said. "I wish Bernie had stayed around long enough to help get you back into the shade."

"It's crawling distance," he said. "I've been crawling everywhere, but it seems to be getting harder. . . ."

"I'd think so. You're becoming weaker and your ankle sure isn't getting any better."

When they were back inside and out of the heat and glare of the sun, Keith stretched his legs in front of him as he leaned back heavily against the wall and sighed. "How do you know about the helicopter, Laura?"

"This is my home ground, Keith. I know everybody who lives around here. The ranches and the land. I knew where to look for you."

"That's a lucky break for me."

"For us both." She knelt beside him. "You don't look very good."

"At this point," he grunted, "just being alive feels good. A man can go without food longer than I thought."

"What happened?"

"Just what you figured. I tried to cross over an arroyo, which turned out to be as deep as my fender. The car stalled. I could hear the water rushing, but it suddenly seemed to get louder. I got out of the car just before a wall of water hit. It looked five feet deep. I couldn't move against it. A big log or something in the water hit my ankle. I was just lucky I was able to stay up and afloat. I thought I was going to drown, but I was tossed sideways when the canyon wall suddenly widened, and I managed to get up to the ledge."

He was speaking with his eyes closed, his head back.

She studied him. "You saw the cottonwood trees, I'll bet. That's why you headed for this place."

"Yeah. There couldn't be big trees like these without water. I had plenty to drink until last night, when it started getting too damned difficult to get down to the stream."

She handed him the canteen, which he accepted gratefully. "What'd you do?" he asked between swallows. "Decide to look where there was water, knowing if I was anywhere in open desert, I'd probably be dead by now?"

She winced. "I knew you were alive."

"You couldn't know that," he said softly.

"I had to believe it, didn't I?"

What she saw in his eyes was no longer only gratitude, and no longer only awe that she was here; it was so much more. Love was in his eyes.

"A helicopter flew over twice. Both times I woke from a deep sleep and couldn't get myself to the door to signal. The town must've looked deserted to them."

Laura touched his face tenderly, brushing back the hair from his eyes. His voice was getting weaker; his eyes remained shut. In spite of his pain, she could see that he was letting go of tension.

"You don't have to try to stay awake any longer. All we can do is wait for Bernie to get back, and it shouldn't take too long if she can find someone at the Harvey ranch. Why don't you just lie down and rest," she urged him gently.

"That's all I've been doing," he said, while he allowed her to coax him down. His head slid onto her lap. His eyes closed once more; keeping them open was too much effort. And sleep rode in through curtains of exhaustion that fell over him.

Laura shifted to get comfortable, her back supported by the wall. It was impossible to keep from touching him as he slept, impossible to keep from feeling the warmth of his skin or the rising of his chest with each living breath.

The erratic flapping of the shutter was the only sound in the silence that surrounded her. How many times, in her childhood days, had she come to this place to enjoy this silence and walk for a few moments with the ghosts of the past? Today those old ghosts no longer mattered. How unpredictable life was, she thought. How strange that we sometimes circle back and begin again. Had she really believed she'd find Keith, or was she only praying? Only playing out some fantasy left from her days of childhood, and by some miracle it had worked?

Why it had worked wasn't important now. Even tomorrow's doubts were pushed back from the forefront of her conscious mind. Keith was safe. For now that was enough; it was everything. She would admit now, only now, how frightened she had been. Only now was she willing to give the desert—her beloved desert—full credit for its wickedness, for its vengeance against all weaker creatures. With the desert for his adversary, Keith was lucky to be alive.

The throb of an engine moved gradually in from over the tops of the trees. "Good job, Bernie!" Laura said aloud.

At the sound of her voice, Keith stirred.

"She did it, Keith! The helicopter is coming in!"

The motor chugs became louder. He'd held on by sheer force of will, determined that there had to be a way out of his dilemma, before Laura had appeared like an angel from heaven. Since then, he'd needed less willpower to fight the pain, knowing some kind of relief was almost within reach. He had walked too much on his injured foot and made it worse. Yesterday morning, trying to hobble on one leg, he had lost his balance and had come down hard on the bad ankle; it had been killing him ever since. He'd never known anything to hurt the way the damned foot was hurting.

"Hold on—I'll be right back," Laura said, pulling her legs gently out from under him.

His head spun when he sat up, so he remained still for some moments, holding his head. The sound of the motor was very loud under whirring blades.

Then Laura was beside him again, with Bernice, urging him to try to get to his feet. A man who was with her moved in, while Laura muttered an introduction, a name he couldn't remember seconds after she'd said it. The stranger offered his support, and Keith found that the man could take most of his weight quite easily. He used his last reserve of strength to help pull himself into the helicopter, where he flopped gratefully into the seat.

Bernice was shouting over the sound of the engine, her red hair blowing. "Jim says there's room for you, Laura! Go with Keith! I'll see you at home!"

Laura gave Bernice a quick, very hard hug and climbed into the helicopter.

"I'd hardly have recognized you, Laura," Jim Harvey said. "You don't come home much anymore."

"It's been a long time, Jim. I'm glad I remembered about your helicopter. There's a landing pad at Northwest Hospital. Do you know how long it'll take to get there?"

"Yup. About forty minutes, as the crow flies."

Forty minutes, Laura thought. Thank heaven for helicopters. Keith was leaning back against the seat, eyes closed, showing no interest whatever in their conversation. Under the noise of the engines, Laura became silent, too, as the huge machine rose up out of the dust of a town that had known no life dramas for more than half a century, until today.

Keith was met by a stretcher, but he refused to be taken into a treatment room until he had called his daughter. It was one o'clock in the afternoon; Justine was at school. His hands were trembling as he lay on a bed in the emergency room holding the phone and waiting for her to be summoned out of class.

She sounded completely out of breath. "Dad? Daddy?"

"It's me, honey. I just wanted to tell you myself I'm okay."

"They said it was you on the phone! I ran all the way to the office! Where were you? Where are you?"

"I'm at Northwest Hospital with a messed-up ankle. I can't talk now, Tina—they're trying to get the phone away from me. But I'll talk to you later, after school, okay?"

"Are you coming home?"

"Yeah, later. I'll be home later. This shouldn't take too long. I'll let you know."

"Okay. Okay. Fantastic. Oh, I'm so ... so ..." She began to sputter into the phone. "Dad?"

"Yeah?"

"I'm so ... glad ... you're back!"

"So am I, baby. So am I. I'll see you very soon."

11

KEITH OPENED HIS EYES to a blur of white ceiling and
sunlight slanting in through window blinds, and Laura
standing over him. He tried to think where he was and
couldn't quite remember; the room was unfamiliar.

She leaned over him. "Keith? Are you awake?"

"Yeah. I'm just...lying here..." he said groggily,
rubbing his hand over his stubbled jaw while he was
trying to orient himself. A hospital room. He didn't
even remember being brought in here.

"You look much better."

"Clean, anyhow, and—" he moved the foot that had
a cast "—properly bandaged. Though I could sure use
a shave. What the hell am I doing here? I've never been
in a hospital and I don't intend to be in one now."

She smiled. "What do you mean, you don't intend to
be? It looks suspiciously like you're already quite settled in."

He grimaced with an almost inaudible oath. "They
tricked me."

"You were in no shape to argue." She touched his
forehead. "They told me they wanted to keep you under observation until tomorrow. You've been through
a lot in the past few days, Keith."

He growled. "They might have consulted me."

"Why fight it? You look like you could use a rest."

"Who can rest in a hospital?"

"You haven't been doing too badly. I think they must have given you a painkiller that knocked you out when they were working on your ankle. You've been sleeping quite soundly for an hour and a half."

"How bad is my ankle? Did they tell you?"

"They didn't tell me much. Only that it's fractured, and the fact that you walked on it a lot and it went untreated for several days made it worse. How is it now? Does it hurt you?"

"Yeah, it hurts. Damn it."

"When are they going to give you something to eat? You must be starving."

"You'd think I'd be hungry, but I'm not. I'm just numb."

"I'll bet they're just waiting until you're awake; and then they'll be assaulting you with gelatin and soup."

He winced. "Is that what you'd give me if I were at your house?"

Her voice softened. "I wish you were at my house. I'd take very good care of you."

He held out his hand to her. "Laura, come here."

"I am here."

"Come closer so I can thank you. I haven't had a chance to thank you."

She smiled as she moved closer to him. "For what?"

"For what, the lady asks. She saves my life and then says for what?"

"Do you know what I went through these past few days, Keith? It was awful. Not knowing if you were alive or dead. Please don't ever scare me like that again."

"One might think," he said softly, urging her toward him, "that you were in love with me."

"One might . . . be right about that . . ." she mumbled as her lips came nearer his.

Strangely, the kiss felt to him much like the first time he had ever kissed her, that night by her front door. Sweet and accepting. Gentle. Unbelievably warm.

"Laura, I love you."

The kiss deepened, strengthened. He threaded his fingers through her soft hair, smelled her perfume, felt happiness move through his tired flesh in the blood that pumped through his heart. Every heartbeat pumping his happiness in loving her, and his luck in finding her. And in her finding him. Behind the fire of their prolonged kiss was the echo of deeper things, some memories already shared, and some still unspoken. Memories yet to be lived.

Holding her hand, Keith sensed a strange tremor of silence in the room, suspended over them. They were not alone.

As if she felt it, too, Laura turned to find Justine standing in the doorway. She merely stood staring at them, a slim figure in jeans and sneakers, a yellow canvas bag thrown over one shoulder. There were tears welling in her eyes.

"Dad?"

"Tina! Sweetheart, how did you get to the hospital?"

Her voice was dry and flat, as if she were in a state of shock. "I got a ride."

Laura stepped aside quickly. Keith held out his arms. Tina hesitated, glanced sideways at Laura, and then, tears streaming, she ran to him. "I thought I'd never see you again!" Her hug was awkward, because he was lying flat on his back in the high bed.

"What is Laura doing here?"

Laura reached out to touch the girl's arm, hesitated and then drew back. "I only dropped in for a minute, Justine. I was just leaving."

"I saw what you were doing!" She turned to her father. "I was so thoroughly hyper. I was, like, dying before I got here. Crazy enough to think how glad you'd be to see me. You weren't even thinking about me! It was totally obvious what you were thinking about!" She was sobbing, deeply hurt.

"You don't understand," he said gently. "Laura is the one who—"

"I'm leaving now," Laura interrupted, backing toward the doorway.

Keith frowned. "Laura . . ."

She smiled. "It's all right. I know you two want to see each other. I understand perfectly."

He knew Laura well enough to see she was upset about Tina coming in at that moment. Undoubtedly, though, she was more upset for Tina than for herself. It had been bad timing, very bad. And she left before he had a chance to protest her leaving. Probably it was for the best; Laura usually knew better than he did what was for the best.

His daughter was gazing at him with wide, tear-filled eyes.

"Why are you crying, honey?"

"Daddy, I was crazy with worry. When they found your car, they thought you'd drowned!"

He looked up at her. "Is that what they told you?"

"No, but, like, they didn't have to say it. I knew. I was never so scared in my life. Where were you? How did they find you?"

"My car got caught in an arroyo in a flash flood. Luckily I got out of the car in time, but I hurt my ankle. I was stranded in the desert, in a ghost town. I'll tell you about it later, when I'm not quite so groggy, okay?"

"Are you all right?"

"I'm fine. Just worn out. A broken ankle, that's all."

She took his hand. "Oh, Daddy, do you know two people drowned in their cars in a flood last week? Not very far from where we thought you were! It was awful not knowing what happened."

"I'm sorry I worried you, Tina. If I'd only been a little more familiar with this country, I don't think it would've happened. I'll know what danger signs to look for next time."

"Next time?" She shivered. "How long do you have to stay in the hospital? When can you come home?"

"I'll come home tomorrow. They can't keep me here longer than tomorrow. Just one more night, and then I'll be home."

"Oh, Daddy, I missed you! I kept thinking, you know, about things we did when I was little. Like the summer at the lake with the boat. Remember?"

He nodded. It had been a long time since she had called him Daddy, and it sounded good to him. It brought back memories of years he had always wanted back. "I kept thinking about that same summer, Tina. You caught your first fish that year."

"Oh, man! And you fell off the water skis when you were supposed to be showing me how to stay on."

He laughed.

But she was crying again. "What if you hadn't come back?"

"I did come back; that's all we have to think about now."

"But . . . Daddy," she sobbed in a high, small voice, "what if you hadn't . . ."

"Don't cry, Tina."

"I was . . . hard on you. You know. Like, I said such awful things before. I kept thinking about that when I thought . . . I thought I might never see you again. I prayed a lot. I wanted another chance."

There were tears in his eyes now. "So did I, Tina."

His words seemed to reassure her. She smiled for the first time. "It will be like those days again, won't it? Like that summer with just you and me together? The way it used to be?"

He held her next to him. "We can never turn time back, honey. Things can never be exactly like they once were."

"Why not?"

"Because . . . for one thing because you're older. . . ."

"No, it's not that! It's because of Laura, isn't it? You want to be with her instead of me?"

"You know damned well how much I want to be with you."

"I saw how you were kissing her. I notice how fast she got up here to see you, how fast you must've called her."

Keith remembered that Laura had interrupted him when he had started to explain to Tina that it was she who had found him. He thought about it now, and decided Laura had a reason for interrupting. This wasn't the best time to tell Tina. She felt left out enough already.

He held her hand. "I called you the second I got to a phone, in the emergency room. Did Kim's mother bring you to the hospital?"

She nodded.

"Is she waiting?"

"No. I told her I was going to stay here with you. I'm not leaving."

"You'll get bored, I'm afraid," he said mildly. "The medication they gave me is making me sleepy, or else it's just that I'm so weak. I'm afraid I'll flake out on you."

"It's okay. Like, I don't care if you go to sleep. Maybe you'll wake up and want something."

He started to protest, to say the nurses were there if he needed anything. But her tearful eyes kept him silent. Tina wanted to be needed, to be needed by him. The most important thing in the world to her right now was that her father needed her. He could hear it in her voice and see it in her eyes and feel it in the mystical bond of love between them. A bond almost forgotten. Until today.

He took her small hand in his large one. "Thanks, Tina. I'll sleep better knowing you're here."

He had no chance to sleep then, because a nurse brought food to him and waited while he ate. Only after he had tasted the soup did he realize how hungry he was. Tina stood back away from the bed a little, patiently waiting.

After the food and another codeine tablet for the pain in his ankle, Keith felt exhaustion overtake him.

"Tina, honey, won't you be bored sitting here? There should be some magazines downstairs...."

"I'm fine, Dad. Don't worry about me, okay?"

Even when he floated on the edge of sleep, Keith could still see the love that shone through the tears in his daughter's eyes. It was a new and different love that kept her presence very near him, even when he slept.

LAURA WAS FILLED with strange and conflicting emotions riding home from the hospital in a taxi. Floating above them all was elation that Keith was safe. Each day of his absence had dawned with a cold sun, an ever-increasing fear that she would never see him again. It was over now. He was home.

But it was not the same. The joy of their first moments together, their first kiss, had been taken from them by Justine's unexpected appearance. It had been a jolting reminder of the tangle of problems that had come between them.

Her thoughts spun into a gnarl of confusion, resentment, helpless frustration and need. Her own need for Keith and for his love. His need for her love. Justine's need to feel secure and wanted. Laura had ached to stay with him at the hospital this afternoon, even if it was only to be there when he slept. To look at him, to touch him and feel the warmth of life in him, after fearing deep inside that she might never feel it again, would have made her completely happy. That was denied her today.

And what of tomorrow?

The route to her home from the hospital spanned the northernmost reaches of the valley, just above the city, along the edges of the Catalina foothills. In this mostly residential area, wide stretches of desert landscape were preserved. It was dense desert here on rolling slopes of the north mountains. Laura stared out of the taxi window on this bright, cloudless September day, so far now from the dusty street of a ghost town. Less than three hours ago there had been only the two of them alone in the whispering desert, with no thoughts of anything but the happiness. It already seemed such a long time ago.

What of tomorrow? The echo persisted and haunted her. Gathering clouds of doubt blew in on shadows of wind that didn't exist in the still afternoon, except in Laura's fretful thoughts. For her, the sun would set tonight in a burning glow of dread.

Laura didn't hear from Keith the following day, or the day after that, except for two brief telephone calls in which he said very little except that he was feeling better and he'd had to see about buying another car. Late in the afternoon of the third day, just after her last client had left, she heard a knock on her office door. Thinking it was Bernice, since the secretary for the offices in her wing had already gone home for the day, she called, "Come on in! I'm free!"

Keith opened the door and hobbled into the room on crutches.

She dropped her pen and stared.

"Hi, Laura," he said softly. "I tried to call this afternoon and was told you were with clients. I found out your last appointment was at four."

She didn't like the strained look around his eyes or the uncertainty in his voice. Something was wrong. "Are you okay?"

"Learning the art of walking with crutches." He plopped awkwardly into an upholstered chair and laid the crutches on the floor beside him. "Lucky I don't use my left foot for driving."

She stared at the cast, then at his face. "I'd like to tell you you look fine and rested, but that wouldn't be entirely true."

"I'm not. I haven't slept worth a damn."

"The cast is uncomfortable?"

"It's not that. It's everything on my mind."

He sat quietly behind a barrier of silence, staring at a painting on the wall. Dread settled over her, nagging and pricking. Whatever it was he had come to say, he didn't want to say it. That much was clear.

"It's Tina, isn't it?" she prompted.

"Yeah."

She waited for him to offer more, but he didn't.

"Tina changed noticeably while you were gone, Keith. She missed you so much it began to dawn on her what it would mean if she lost you. I think she did a lot of thinking about you, and realized that you had always been there for her."

"Yeah," he agreed. "She has changed. I'm amazed how much. And I know part of it's because of you. She said you and she had talked."

"A little. I get the feeling she'd like to be friends with me, but she can't allow herself to do it because I'm such a threat to her relationship with you."

He nodded. "You are very much a threat to her, Laura. She's terrified of you. I mean of my . . . loving you."

"Her walking in on us at the hospital was the worst thing that could have happened. I knew that at the time, but it was too late. Nothing either of us could have said would have made matters any better."

"She feels left out, as if she's the outsider."

The coil of dread within Laura was growing with each passing moment. Why, she wondered, did the world have to be so complicated? Wasn't love enough? "Tina feels even more left out now when she wants so badly to build a closer relationship with you. She really does want to be closer to you, doesn't she?"

"Yeah. Nothing like a helluva scare to change the direction of one's life. Tina is actually afraid to be alone now. This morning when I woke up, she was lying on the foot of my bed sound asleep. With a stuffed teddy bear in her arms."

"It was your first night home. I'm sure that insecurity won't last."

"It's here now, though, and it shakes me."

She would not look at his eyes. Something in her knew that whatever was there right now, she didn't want to see, not ever.

He lapsed into silence again. *It's the calm before the storm*, she thought. Her stomach was in a tight knot, and her throat felt as though she couldn't swallow. And she was certain Keith was paler than he was when he had hobbled in.

He shifted uncomfortably in the chair. "It's killing me to tell you this, Laura, but it just isn't going to work. It just . . . I can't figure any way to make it work."

"You mean you and me."

He nodded miserably. "There's no way to half do it. I just have to make it a clean break. A final break. I feel I haven't any choice."

She stared at him, unable to speak.

"I've let my daughter down too many times. She's at such an important place in her life right now. I don't have to tell you what a hell of a year it's been for her. And now this past week on top of it all. If I let her down this time, I couldn't live with myself."

After a long, agonizing pause, he said, "Please say something."

Her voice almost cracked. "I don't know what to say."

"This is the hardest thing I've ever had to do in my life. I wish I had a choice, but I haven't. Tina just can't handle my having a woman in my life."

"You've discussed it?"

"A little. It's not easy to discuss it with her."

"Why not? What does Tina do when you bring up my name?"

"She just . . . she cries."

Laura nodded to show his answer didn't surprise her. Finally she said, "You know I think the world of your daughter. She's a very special person to me. I know her fairly well, and I know she's very sincere in her feelings, but nevertheless, Keith, you are being manipulated."

"Yes, I know it. But Tina's so damned sensitive and determined. If I alienate her right now, there's no telling what could happen to her. She could run away, maybe get into drugs. You know the trouble she's capable of getting into."

"Anything to punish you for caring about someone else when she wants you all to herself."

"Yes. But it's my last chance to get her life straightened out and on the right track. I have to do that, Laura. For once in my life I'm going to do what a father is supposed to do—I'm going to put my daughter first."

She looked at the floor. "You've thought about this carefully, haven't you?"

"I've thought of nothing else for the past two days. And it's killing me. I feel as if something inside me is dying. I had actually begun to have fantasies of . . ." He shook his head as if to rid himself of the thoughts inside him.

"Fantasies of you and me being together?"

He winced at her directness. "It was only a dream. It can't ever happen."

By now she was fighting to hold back tears. Keith was giving up love, giving up a partnership, giving up a future dream . . . and tearing her own dreams to shreds at the same time. It wasn't fair. It was so damned unfair!

But it was no use trying to talk him out of it. He had weighed everything and made up his mind. As far as Keith was concerned, his decision was the only decision he could make. She knew nothing she could say would change his mind, and she decided not to voice her concern for the long-term deleterious effects on Justine of being able to manipulate her father so adroitly.

He reached for the crutches on the floor and struggled to his feet. She rose, too. Her eyes were stinging, but she still struggled not to cry. Not in front of him, at least. It was bad enough already.

He hesitated as though he hadn't said all there was to say, and as if he didn't want to face her, because he looked away. When he turned back to her his own eyes had filled with tears. "Laura . . ."

She bit her lip, almost reeling with the pain.

His deep voice was husky with emotion. "I didn't want it like this—God knows I didn't. Do you...can you understand?"

She touched his shoulder, trying hard to force herself to accept what some part of her knew she would never accept. "I can see why you've come to this conclusion. And I'll admit I don't know any other answer...at least not right now. It just...just..." Her tears, unsuppressible because of the sight of his, shone in her eyes. "I don't agree, but I do understand why you...yes, damn it, I understand."

"I can't build my own happiness on my daughter's pain."

"Yes," she whispered. "I know."

Light from the window brightened the glaze of tears in his eyes. "I love you, Laura. But don't wait for me. It isn't fair to you. Go on with your life without me. I can't come back."

"Keith . . ." she whispered, crying. It was not a plea; it was only his name. One last time. His name left in a husk of shattered dreams.

Balancing on the crutches, he bent to kiss her forehead softly, unhurriedly, before he turned to leave. He didn't look back.

With burning eyes, Laura stared at the closed door. That tender kiss on her forehead was his goodbye. He hadn't been able to bring himself to actually say the word aloud, and neither had she. Goodbye was a forever word. It was enough that the word he couldn't speak was in his eyes, in the shine of his tears.

For an unmeasured time she stood in the spot where he had left her. Inside the awful silence was her tearing heart. Silence was such loneliness after the joy of being loved.

ON HER TERRACE, loneliness lingered like the darkness that filled the night sky. She could still feel the presence of Keith here. His velvet voice, the scent of his aftershave, his touch all lingered in the folds of her memory. Loving him hurt so much. Reaching for him when he was not there. Longing for him when he would no longer be there.

Bitterness settled in like mist, becoming heavier as the hours passed, becoming resentment that two people's lives should be shattered by the jealousy of a third. Tina would eventually go on to find her own way in the world and her own chance for happiness, probably never realizing the sacrifice her father had made for her out of choice. Keith was wrong, she thought. But trying to put herself in his place, Laura was reminded of the commitment he'd made the day he'd decided his daughter would be better off with him than with adoptive parents. He felt he'd failed Tina and he'd go to any length to make up for that; he'd just proved it.

So his happiness was spoiled, and hers as well, because Tina's selfishness defied even the slightest compromise. And because Tina had learned where her father was most vulnerable: his responsibilities as a parent. Laura felt overwhelmed by how unfair Tina was to her father. Keith wasn't being fair, either, to just walk away.... But he had walked away, fair or not, and nothing she could do would change his mind. Tina could change his mind, but she wouldn't; Tina was thinking only of herself.

A florist delivered a bouquet of sweet summer flowers to her that evening. And a note in Keith's handwriting. "A small token of gratitude for saving my life, and for making that wretched life really worth living for a while. And for all the memories you gave me. With love, Keith." For a long time she held the flowers. But when she finally put them down, she didn't want to look at them.

On the small patch of grass near her swimming pool three cottontail rabbits were grazing in the last gray light of day. She watched them as the shadows closed in around her and enshrouded her in darkness.

12

HE SCARCELY THOUGHT OF AUTUMN because the desert itself had so few thoughts of the changing season. But on some early mornings, crossing the palm-lined campus, he thought of the bronze and yellow autumns of Michigan where he had been a child. Blue lakes with high brown reeds and silver marshes, and softly moving patterns of migrating birds in flight overhead. So long ago.

Crippled and illogical autumn passed. The sun softened. Summer grasses dried. New winter grass sprouted bright green over the campus lawns. Days hardened into brittle splinters of passing time. Chill of December nights hung in the first shadows of early twilight and lingered well past dawn. And he thought of Laura. Always Laura.

He lived with his decision because he had to, certain it had been the right thing to do. Tina's life had turned around; she had shed her bitterness toward him even before he'd returned from his lost days in the desert. In the time since, she had accepted his love, and this acceptance had made the difference.

He saw her less and less as time passed and she glided through her busy days with the flurry and rush of youth. New classes for the January term. New friends. Afterschool sports. Dates. And then a special date, a special boy.

To encourage her enthusiasm for her expanding world, Keith took her to a concert in December, and to the opera in January, the latter because their drama teacher had read aloud rave reviews of *MacBeth*, and Tina and Kim had begged to go.

He had fidgeted restlessly through the first half of the opera while the girls sat spellbound. At intermission he excused himself and went to the lobby for a drink.

Standing aside, feeling more out of place than anywhere he'd ever been, Keith gulped Scotch and looked around him at the glittering crowd. That was when he saw her.

Laura in a green silk suit, looking more beautiful than he remembered, was standing in a group of people across the room. She was smiling, listening more than talking.

Feeling strange, as though this place and this vision of Laura were something he was dreaming rather than living, Keith stood hypnotized behind the milling crowd and watched her. The familiar tossing of her head. Her smile. Her radiance setting her apart from every other woman in the room.

Something, perhaps the feeling of eyes on her, made Laura look up. Her smile vanished when she caught sight of Keith across the room, and their eyes met. Hesitantly he raised his glass in greeting. She said a few words to those nearest her before she broke from the group and came toward him. By the time she had reached his side, her smile had returned.

"Keith! What a surprise to see you! And here, of all places."

"The proverbial fish out of water," he said.

"Are you enjoying the opera?"

"I can't stand it. But Tina thinks it's great."

"You brought Tina? How is she?"

"She's fine. Working hard at school. She's . . . happy, Laura."

"Good. That's very good news. And you?"

"Me?"

She was absolutely composed, he observed, with just the right casual lilt in her voice. But he couldn't miss the sadness in her eyes; it was a sadness he didn't want to see.

"Has your ankle healed okay?"

"Oh, yeah, my ankle's fine. How are you these days?"

She shrugged and smiled. "Well, you know . . . busy. I was pleased to see they arrested the man who attacked me in the library parking lot. The police must have asked you to identify him."

"Yeah. In a lineup. They say he'll go to trial next month. He could save himself some trouble by confessing."

He took a great gulp of Scotch and smiled down at her. "Is it a good opera, Laura? Tell me so if anybody asks I'll know what to say."

Because of her sad eyes, Keith gazed at the long strand of pearls she wore around her neck instead of her face. Finally, however, her silence made him look up again. She was staring at him with an expression he couldn't read.

"Yes," she answered finally. "It's a very good opera, by far the best of the season."

He grinned. "I'll think about that, then, while I'm trying to sit through the second half." But what he really meant was he would be thinking about her.

"It's been . . . it's nice to see you, Keith."

"Same here. You look terrific."

She backed away, hesitated, then smiled again and teased, "You can trust me—it's a fine opera."

"Right." He smiled back and turned toward the balcony stairs.

The agony of seeing Laura again was made worse by this place and by having to sit through the second half of the opera knowing she was in the concert hall somewhere out of sight, maybe thinking of him. The jolt of seeing her was far worse than he'd imagined it would be. It was as if the clock had turned back to the day in her office when he had left her, as if it had been only hours since then. As if he could laugh and put his arm around her and pretend the past four and a half months had never been.

But it wasn't so, he reminded himself with furious frustration. He had walked out, and since that day she hadn't heard a word from him. He'd been true to his word and left forever. There was no going back, no pretending it hadn't happened.

Tina and Kim chattered excitedly about the costumes and the elaborate stage settings as they walked out into the welcome cold of the night air. He caught sight of the shimmering green of Laura's skirt once again in the crowd. She was walking several yards ahead of them in the thick of the crowd with her hand on the arm of an escort. Keith blanched. She was here with another man! His mind raced with wild, irrational fury. A great, painful rush of jealousy, emotional and physical hurt, made his temples throb. He was scarcely aware of the clenching of his fists that pushed the powerful muscles of his arms against the fabric of his shirt. His step quickened with an illogical kind of urgency. He'd find out, and find out fast, what the hell was going on! Just who the devil did this guy think he was...?

Moving past the shimmering fountains at close to a running pace, Keith felt a hard tugging on his coat. He heard Tina's frantic query.

"What's wrong, Dad? Where are you going? Damn it, wait for us!"

His daughter's voice was like a rush of cold water, dousing him with the reality of the present. Keith blinked the pain of hot rage from his eyes while he fought to gain control of that rage. He stopped and turned slowly toward Tina and Kim with a blank stare, as if trying to figure out where he was.

He swallowed, remembering. A flood of agony crashed over him so heavily that he felt he had to gasp to keep from drowning.

The man with Laura was tall and thin and blond and smiling. There were two couples; the other woman was Bernice. She kept turning around to Laura and her date, talking with great animation as Bernice always did. The crowd gradually closed in between them while Keith fought his hurt and fury. He could feel perspiration in his still-clenched fists.

Tina's hand was again tugging at his arm. "What's wrong?"

"Nothing's wrong!" he answered sharply.

"Hey! Didn't you like the opera?"

"What?"

"I said, did you dig the opera?"

Reality was difficult for him to grasp in the wake of shock. He inhaled a great breath of the cold night air and tried to pull his voice back to normal.

"Did you?"

"Oh, man, yeah! Except, you know, for not understanding the words."

"Well, as long as you enjoyed it."

They were crossing the street, under bright streetlamps, Tina in the middle, and Kim struggling to keep up. Tina looked up at him and repeated, "What's wrong, Dad?"

"I told you, nothing."

"You look sorta funny. Like devastated. You didn't hate it that much, did you?"

"I'm tired, Tina. I'm just . . . tired."

It was his own fault, he told himself, feeling the full force of defeat. What choice had he left Laura? It wasn't as if he'd lost her love—he had thrown it away. He'd taken the most precious gift he'd ever had and crushed it, tossed it up to the wind. And it was gone. All but the poignant memories, which wouldn't ever blow away, not ever. Laura had found a new life now, just as he'd told her to do.

In their living room, after Kim had been dropped off at home, Tina asked, "Do you want me to make some coffee?"

"No, thanks."

She tried to get his attention, but he wouldn't look at her. He threw his coat over a chair. "What's with you, Dad? Something is bugging you to the max. Don't deny it cuz I know you."

"Do you, Tina?" he asked in a voice edged with bitterness. "Do you know me?"

She hesitated with new concern. "I know when you're massively bugged."

"You're right. I'm massively bugged."

"What's wrong? Geez, if the opera—"

"The opera has nothing to do with anything."

"What, then? Why won't you even look at me? Come on, tell me!"

Loosening his necktie, he turned and met her quizzical gaze. "I saw Laura at the opera."

Tina blinked and paled slightly. "Oh."

He threw down the tie and poured himself a drink at the counter that separated the living room from the kitchen.

Behind him Tina said in a small voice, "I thought you were over Laura."

"Why would you think that?"

"Well...it's been... Like, you never mention her...."

Keith knocked back a large swallow of whiskey and was silent.

His daughter's voice hardened. "Dad, you agreed Laura was coming between us. She wanted to take you away from me."

"Don't be an idiot, Tina. That was the very last thing Laura wanted."

"Yes, she did! She wanted you for herself!"

He glared at her. "I thought you were starting to grow up. Right now you sound like a five-year-old."

Slumping into a chair with a pout on her face, Tina challenged him. "Well, you sound like you want her back."

"It's too late for that. What's done is done. But I think it's time you started looking at our relationship—yours and mine—with a little more adult perspective. You might start with defining the boundaries of possessiveness now that you're wanting more freedom in your own life. There's a difference between protectiveness and possessiveness. You'd better start thinking about it."

Worry filled her eyes as she looked up at him in uncomfortable silence. "You're not going back to Laura? You promise?"

"Damn it, Tina! Have you heard anything I just said? No, I'm not going back to Laura because I can't! But since you keep bringing her into this conversation, and since you persist in your childish resentment of her, I think I ought to tell you something about Laura. I might not be alive today if it weren't for her. It was Laura who found me in the desert after the search parties had abandoned me."

"What? Laura found you?"

His only response was to take another drink from his glass.

"Why didn't you ever tell me?"

"It was her idea not to tell you. She thought you might resent it and be more threatened by her than you were already."

"Oh, like, super! Treating me like a child!"

"You were acting like a child."

A shine of tears surfaced in her eyes. "You were with her so much . . . and I needed you."

"Of course you did. Everyone, including Laura, understood that. We needed each other, you and I. We needed a chance. I left Laura so you and I would have that chance; it wasn't because Laura wanted to take me away from you. She wanted . . . us both."

"Well, we didn't need her." She looked at the floor and shuffled her feet, while the silence of the room came down over them. Finally she asked softly, "How did she know where to find you . . . in that ghost town where you were?"

"I'm still not sure, except that she grew up in that area of southern Arizona and knew the terrain well. She worked out a theory about what road I'd be on where the floods had washed over the road."

"You should've told me."

He shrugged. "You didn't want to hear anything like that then. What I expect of you now, though, Tina, is to be more—" he rubbed the back of his neck as if it were stiff "—more charitable. And more realistic."

She squinted at him, scowling. "Cripes, are we going through all this because you happened to see Laura at the opera?"

His stare was piercing. "That's what triggered it, yeah. I won't pretend anymore that Laura isn't important to me. Your well-being was more important to me at the time I stopped seeing Laura than my own was— or hers. You needed me and I was there, and I'm glad I was there. I wouldn't change that. You're fine and happy now, which proves it was the right thing for me to do. But you're also getting older by the day, and I won't put up with stupid comments about how Laura wanted to take me away from you. It isn't true, and you're adult enough to know it isn't true. Laura did a lot for you and cared very deeply about you, and you know it."

"Are you trying to lay a guilt trip on me or something?"

"Hell, no, Tina, I'm just leveling with you. You said the other day you want us to have an adult relationship. Good. I want that, too. This is the only way to begin. Starting over with honesty. You asked what was bothering me tonight and I told you. It was seeing

Laura. Now you can accept that for what it is. It will be a long time and maybe never before I forget Laura. So give me that, and try seeing something from my point of view for once. It's called growing up."

LAURA PULLED her bedroom curtains tightly shut that night, so that she couldn't see the moon. It shone white through the desert air and threw eerie shadows over everything. She'd always imagined the desert was haunted on nights of the full moon. And when the white light shone in, her bedroom was haunted, too, by the presence of the man she loved. It was haunted by her memories of other nights, nights of love, nights with Keith.

Time didn't heal the aching. It was as strong now as it had been the day he'd left her. And tonight, seeing him again . . . She sat in bed, her face buried in her hands, and whispered his name time and time again into the darkness.

KEITH DRAGGED through the following day under the yoke of depression. Seeing Laura again had shaken him out of his state of limbo, forcing him to yield to the reality of his longing for her. Time was supposed to make it easier. It hadn't. Time was supposed to be a cure for everything. It wasn't. Time was only an opponent who won by trickery and a false reputation. Time had brought another man into Laura's life.

Realizing that was like receiving a blow to his solar plexus, knocking all the air out of him. He slammed and growled through his day, breathing in the stale air of regret. Sharp pains stabbed his heart.

He was at home that night trying to concentrate on a file of science papers when Justine whirled into the room singing, "Dad, look what I found on sale today! I've been dying for this sweater, and I found it reduced to half price!"

He looked up from his work. "I like the color. Pink looks good on you. Are you going out?"

"Yeah. John will be here any minute. He's neat, don't you think, Dad? I mean, he's one of the main hunks at school."

"So I've heard."

"Well, don't you think so?"

"I wouldn't know."

"You're grouchy! You been a grouch all day. Come on, grouch, you like John, don't you? You said you did."

"Is it important for me to like him?"

"Sure! Like, naturally it is!"

Keith rubbed his chin and looked at her in silence for a moment. "I like him fine. Just as long as he doesn't keep you out past eleven tonight."

A car pulled up in the drive.

"That's him! I won't be late. We're going to the ice rink. Oh, my skates!" She dashed into her room and back out again swinging a pair of ice skates and a small shoulder bag. Hurriedly she kissed her father's cheek. "Bye, Dad."

She had almost reached the door in response to the ringing bell, when she turned back and gazed at him for some seconds, her smile gone. "Dad, why do you stay home so much? You're getting positively dull!"

Within moments he was alone with only the silence of the apartment and the internal growling of his own anger. Not anger at Tina, but at himself. He'd put his own life on hold for her and it had been all right, maybe even good, for a while. But now, since their heated discussion after the opera, Tina surely realized more fully what he'd done. She was even telling him he was carrying it too far!

His life had been work and nothing else for the past four, almost five, months. Tina was right; he was getting dull. He felt dull. But the incentive to change this wasn't there, especially after seeing Laura last night. He hadn't known how much he missed her until then. Hadn't allowed himself to think how much he'd thrown away.

There was no use thinking about it now, though. It was too late. Keith threw down the paper he was reading and went to find his jogging shoes. He needed to work off some frustration.

A FEW EVENINGS LATER he was sitting with Tina in the living room, drinking colas and eating popcorn while they worked. She looked up from her books. "Dad, I can't do this gnarly damned report. I have to have like information on Robert Browning. We're supposed to find stuff in the library and list our sources. Would you take me over there? I promise I won't dink around. I'll hurry."

"I guess so, if it's important."

"It is. This is a special report that's going to guar-
antee me an A in English."

He looked at his watch. "Come on, then. Get your
jacket. The library probably closes at nine."

"Oh, cripes! It's all dark!" Tina whined as they drove
into the parking lot of the nearest public library. "The
library must be closed Monday night! I've had it! I'm
doomed! What am I gonna do, Dad?"

"Don't panic, Tina. We can go over to the university
library."

She made a terrible face. "That library is so big it
thoroughly grosses me out! I could never find anything!"

He smiled. "You can get all the help you need in that
main reference room. Anyway, it sounds to me as if
that's what your assignment is all about. You're supposed to get acquainted with where things are in a library. Give it a try, and if you get stuck I'll help you."

He left her in the reference room on the main floor
and went downstairs to a reading room. It was a large
room that smelled of ink. The walls were lined with
newspapers in racks, hundreds of them, from cities in
the U.S. and around the world. Keith settled himself in
a chair to read an issue of the *Wall Street Journal* and
wait for Tina.

Several people, mostly university students, were in
the room. Some were reading, some milled about the
displays, some were looking at microfilm.

He glanced up from his reading after a time and, in a rush of surprise, lost his breath. Across the room, Laura was standing between the racks of newspaper displays searching through the papers. Her back was toward him; she seemed quite absorbed in the search. He couldn't believe it: twice in little more than a week he'd seen her. And here in the library where they had first been brought together that strange, hot night last August.

For half a minute he watched her, or tried to. People walking back and forth in the wide room between them sometimes blocked his view of her. He felt strangely detached, as if she were on a movie screen and he were only a spectator. Laura seemed so near and yet so far away, so real and at the same time only a dream—a dream forbidden him. His pulse raced; his stomach quivered. He sat as if frozen.

She looked up and broke the spell. As from a dike, a great rush of agonizing emotions was released from his body. The woman was not Laura! Blood rushed to Keith's head; his fists clenched tightly with frustration. His disappointment was almost crushing.

I'm losing my mind, he thought. *I'm haunted by her. I'm going to start seeing her everywhere, like a ghost.* He couldn't live that way. It was unacceptable.

No longer interested in finishing the article he'd started, he sat staring at the spot where the woman had been. When she'd turned around and walked to the exit, he had realized she didn't really look like Laura at all.

He clamped his teeth together and got up, pacing restlessly around the perimeters of the room until he could no longer stand the atmosphere there. Moments later he found himself alone in the wide, silent hallway.

At the top of the stairs he saw Tina, notebook in her hand.

"I was just coming downstairs to look for you."

His heartbeat had returned to normal, but the sense of urgency hadn't left him—an awful, haunting feeling of something wrong, something terribly wrong. A kind of grief he could feel but never quite touch. Emptiness and urgency together, but becoming more emptiness than urgency as the flow of adrenaline slowed. The woman was not Laura. Laura was not part of his world anymore.

"Are you finished with your English paper? Did you find what you needed?"

"Yeah, I got it. One of the librarians helped me."

"Good. Let's get out of here, then."

She looked up at him as he walked swiftly toward the door. "Hey, is something wrong? What's the rush?"

"Let's just go, Tina. All right?"

"Like, you look a little riled, Dad...."

He didn't answer, but pushed his way through the turnstiles and out the front door into the cold February night.

On the top of the slope he hesitated, again remembering the night he had met Laura, when he had stood on this same spot and watched her walk under the streetlamp to her car. For a moment he stared at the glow of white light under the lamp. In his mind he could see the soft flow of her pink skirt, the shine of her blond hair. The ache throbbed all through him. All the illusions brought on by his crazed and sightless regret weren't going to change the fact that he had lost her.

In the car Tina turned to him. "You're being a massive zombie, Dad. What's with you?"

"I'm in a bad mood."

"No kidding? Like, what else is new? You've been in a stinking mood all week. The house has been zombie city."

"Maybe it has. You said yourself I'm getting dull."

"Yeah, well, tonight you're dull to the utter max."

"Thanks a lot." He stared at the lights of oncoming cars as he drove and thought of Laura. Was she at home tonight? Did she think of him on these cold winter nights sometimes? Or was she busy with the new man in her life, the man on whose arm she'd left the opera? It wasn't easy to think about her; until now he'd forcefully stopped himself from doing it. But analyzing his emotions, his anticipation, when he'd thought she was there in the same room at the library, he knew he missed her now even more than he had. His failure to admit that was badly messing up his life.

Something had to change. Something had to give. Keith knew when he'd had enough, when he couldn't stoically take it any longer. He glanced across at his daughter and decided to test her.

"Dull to the utter max, huh? That's a bad prognosis, Tina. Maybe I'll try to do something about that. We'll get the cabin up at Pine Top this weekend and do some skiing."

She gazed at him in horror. "Dad! You know this weekend is the Sweetheart Dance at school!"

"Sure, I know that. But this is more important. It'll be great, Tina, just the two of us and the snow. Maybe we'll rent a snowmobile."

"Come on! I'm going to the dance, Dad! I promised John. We're double-dating with Pam and Andy, and you said I could buy the blue taffeta dress! It's only, like, the best dance of the year. We're getting *corsages*!"

"But I want to go to the mountains, Tina."

She stared wide-eyed. "But I don't!"

"You don't want to be with me?"

"Well, I . . ." she sputtered. "Well, but . . ."

"But you'd rather be with your friends."

"Like, cripes, Dad! Everybody wants to be with their friends!"

"Does everybody include me?"

She gazed at him with questioning, suspicious eyes. He was looking at the road, not at her. Silence fell again, uncomfortably.

Finally, he spoke. "I suppose John would be disappointed if you broke your date for the dance."

"Only, like, thoroughly devastated. He's renting a tuxedo. He's *reserved* it."

His eyebrows raised. "A tux for a high school dance?"

"Like I said. It's a main event."

"And our ski weekend wouldn't be?"

She lapsed into a pout.

"I wasn't too fond of your boyfriend when I first met him. I suppose I was being unfair about my objections."

"Unfair to the max! You were awful. You didn't trust me or anything."

"That's true. But I didn't forbid you to go with him, did I? I gave you a chance. I gave him a chance."

"Yeah, well, see? And now you like him."

"Yes. Now I like him. And I trust you." He was stopped at a stoplight and looked over at her and spoke in a softer voice. "Even if I didn't trust you, Tina, I wouldn't have the right to run your life, would I? You have a right to live your own life."

She smiled happily and nodded.

"And what about me? Do I have the same freedom, Tina?"

She wrinkled her nose. "Like what?"

"I'm talking about the freedom to live my own life. The freedom to sometimes prefer being with my friends, just as you do. Without getting a lot of sulking and back talk."

"Like, when did I ever do that?"

He smiled, relaxing. "Once you did that. When you were younger."

13

KEITH UNLOCKED THE DOOR of their apartment. "I'm going out for a while, Tina. Be sure you lock up before you go to bed."

She turned on the lights and set her books on the table. "Where are you going this late?"

"Just out."

"But where?"

He gazed steadily at her. "I'm going out to see a friend."

She shrugged. "Oh...sure...right." Kicking off her shoes and fidgeting with her hair, she seemed greatly bothered. "Dad? Is it okay about the skiing? I mean not going this weekend? I mean, the dance..."

He smiled. "It's okay. You have your priorities—I know that."

She nodded thoughtfully, uncertainly, kicking her shoes under the table.

Keith knew his daughter was beginning to suspect she'd been set up, though she didn't know exactly how or why he'd picked tonight to verbally demarcate the borders of their relationship. It was less negotiation than command; he was cornering her with treaty terms she herself had helped design.

He had no way of knowing for sure whether the squint of her eyes and the uncertainty in her voice were signs of hesitant agreement or remnants of defiance.

Kissing her gently on the forehead, he said, "Leave a light burning for me, okay?"

She looked up at him, her forehead creased in a frown, her eyes filled with unasked questions. She nodded slowly in response and watched him leave.

FOR NEARLY HALF AN HOUR Keith drove aimlessly, with the car window wide open. He needed to think, needed the cold winter wind in his face to clear his head. The three-quarter moon was bright, its silver light throwing an eerie glow over the shadows of the desert. He had headed north, toward the Santa Catalinas.

What had happened at the library—the illusion of Laura there—had shaken him. His love had somehow built on itself, intensified to overload and finally exploded in disturbing tricks of his mind. And the thought of Laura with another man caused his jaw to clench and his knuckles to whiten on the steering wheel. This was hell, he concluded, riddled with self-hate and the pain of regret. He couldn't live like this.

A plan began to form. First he'd get hold of himself. He would have to appear calm and in control before he confronted Laura and found out what was going on in her life now. He needed to learn if he had a chance— any chance at all—to undo what he had done by leaving her.

They'd chat, casually, like friends. Maybe he'd ask her if she wanted to have a drink with him tomorrow.

He'd go slowly and carefully. Because he'd hurt her badly and because of the other man in the picture he had to go slowly and carefully. He repeated the phrase to himself over and over. It was going to take patience and finesse to win Laura back if indeed it wasn't too late. She might already be in love with whoever the hell that tall guy was.

It was hard for Keith to imagine Laura in love with another man after what they'd shared. It had been so incredibly special. Keith pounded the steering wheel in festering frustration. What a damned fool he was! How could Laura trust him now, after he'd hurt her so?

"Casual," he said aloud. "Just be casual. You're only there to apologize for being a fool. Remember that. Just to apologize. And don't stay. Five minutes to apologize, ask if she'll have a drink sometime, or dinner at the most...the very most. Patience is the key. Just take it slow and easy. Just feel out the situation very carefully. Very carefully."

He turned onto the dark, winding street where Laura lived. There were few streetlights here; the desert stood silent in the chill of night. He wondered what she would do when she saw him. For all he knew she wasn't alone in her house tonight.

His pulse was racing as he pulled into her circular drive. Her porch light was on, as if she was expecting him. Or expecting someone. Repeating the word "Patience!" to himself over and over, he got out of the car as slowly as he could and walked toward her door.

Her entry garden flooded suddenly with bright light and the front door opened. She stood in the light of the doorway; the gold of her hair shone in the glow like a halo. She took a step or two forward, onto the stone path, watching him approach out of the darkness.

Laura said nothing, only stood mutely as he walked toward her. Keith paused in the frame of the open wrought-iron gate, stunned by her beauty, as he always was. For several seconds he stood as silently as she, unable to see her eyes in the shadows.

Finally his voice cracked through the frosty, ragged darkness. "Laura, if I've lost you it's my own fault. But I don't want to lose you. I want you back!"

Oh, God, he thought with a sinking heart in the silent moments that followed. What had happened to his plan, his determination, his patience? Laura only stared at him, as if she could find no words to respond to such an outburst.

Then he saw the small gleam of tears in her eyes when she turned sideways and then back to him.

"I want you back," he repeated, trying to hide the fear choking him because of her silence.

Finally her voice trembled on the night chill. "Keith . . . you never lost me."

He stared. She stared back. The sounds of the desert closed around them. Keith, slowly comprehending, slowly translating those five small words, moved forward through the shimmering silence to take her in his arms.

A FIRE WAS BURNING in Laura's fireplace. The orange-pink glaze filled the room with soft, flickering light. Keith had lit the fire, and she had poured wine for them.

They had sat in the warmth for several minutes, saying very little because there was too much to say. Who could begin, and where? Or had everything already been said, without the saying?

As quiet moments passed with the cracking and popping of a winter fire, Laura's emotions spun and scattered and rolled back somehow into focus, crystallizing. She was left with Keith's presence and new insights into the mysteries of human love.

He set down his glass, raised his eyes to her and said her name. He invited her into his waiting arms as though he'd never left her.

His kiss was memory and promise together, but more promise than memory. There had been so many times, alone, when she had longed for the touch of him again. How many tears had she shed, believing he was gone from her forever? And now, so suddenly, almost before she had caught her breath, he had returned. Suddenly and unplanned. How was it possible that things could have changed so much? And yet they had.

As if he reading her thoughts, Keith brushed his fingers through her hair. "I've made love to you in warm moonlight, but never in firelight."

"Now there's firelight."

His lips brushed softly against her forehead, her cheeks, her lips, her throat. On the outside of her clothes, his fingers caressed lightly over her neck and her breasts, and she shivered in new anticipation.

"Are you hot in your sweater?"

"Yes," she answered. "Are you?"

"Very." He raised up and pulled the heavy white sweater over his head. Before he had a chance to help her, Laura had thrown her own sweater aside.

Sprawling on his back, he pulled her down beside him playfully onto the soft carpet. He ran his hands over her bare shoulders and smiled, "I hate to tell you how much sleep I lost after I saw you that night with another man . . . Bernice's brother?"

She shrugged and smiled. "That's what I said. Bernice's brother."

"Tell me about Bernice's brother."

"Mark has two ex-wives."

"Only two? What else?"

"There isn't anything else that I know of."

"You went to the opera with him."

"I've gone to several operas with Mark. He loves opera."

"Does he love you?"

"Of course not. He's just . . . Bernie's brother."

"There has to be something wrong with any man who doesn't love you."

She held his warm hand against her cheek. "I had no idea you were so jealous."

"Neither did I."

"Laura . . ." he began, while his fingers tenderly caressed her cheek. "You were true to me. Why?"

"It never occurred to me not to be."

"But I left you."

"Did you?"

"Yes. No. Part of me never left you." He was lying on his back on the white carpet, looking up at her, his eyes reflecting the soft light of the fire, his fingertips caressing her throat. "But I told you I left, so why were you true to me?"

"Because I love you."

He blinked. She saw him swallow with his lips still parted. "Laura . . ."

When she realized he wasn't going to say more, she lowered her head toward him and smiled softly. "Were you true to me?"

"Yes."

"Even when you left me?"

"Yes."

"Why?"

"Because I love you. And I was a fool to think time could ever change that."

Braced on her elbow, she smiled into his eyes, ruffling his hair.

He said, "You're very forgiving, after I turned my back on you the way I did, not talking it over, just turning my back."

"You were up against a wall, Keith. I understood that part."

"I didn't want to hurt you. I hate myself for hurting you."

She smiled softly. "I don't think it would take much time in this firelight to make us forget our days apart."

"This fire is making me hot."

"Yes, so you said. It isn't a truly blazing fire yet."

"Oh, yes it is. I want to take off my clothes."

"Then by all means do."

Seconds later she was gazing at him dreamily. "You always seem so comfortable naked."

"It's the natural way to be, isn't it?"

"Well . . . not everywhere . . ."

"With you, though."

"I'm inclined to agree," she said, unbuttoning the waist of her skirt.

Glow of golden flames on white skin. Velvet throw pillows from the couch. Whispers from open, eager lips, flush of heat with every new and hungry kiss. Warm caresses, insatiable longing.

"You'll never know," he said, "how much I've wanted you. . . ."

"I know about wanting." Her words came distorted on a moan as his hands moved along the insides of her thighs, his lips warmed her breasts. She closed her eyes and let the pulse of her own pounding blood find the pulse of his. His chest against hers, his breath, sweet and cool against her cheek, his lips on her closed eyelids. His hands wandering, gently exploring.

Then less gently than possessively. Hands that lay claim to her, hands to avow that no part of her was forbidden him. Hands to advance the path for his lips to follow.

In those moments she did not know how to separate her heart from her body, or her mounting passion from her all-consuming love for him. It was all the same, all spinning together, spinning wilder and faster into a storm so magical she could not yet think of the cloudburst, only of the wild gales that caught and held them.

She forbade him nothing. Nothing of the full, ripe harvest of her arousal. He accepted. He took.

He gave. More and more.

And she, in shivers of acceptance, abandoned herself to the luxuriousness of his lips.

"Keith . . ."

His response was a soft moan, ever so soft, as his fingers glided over her body until he found her hand and took it in his own. His fingers pressed hard and harder against hers, silent bonding, silent reassurance, while he urged her closer and closer into the heart of the tempest.

She writhed, out of control, grasping for his shoulder. "Oh . . ."

He understood.

His moves were so graceful that Laura scarcely felt the shifting of lips, ease of skillful hands staying . . . staying . . . until she found herself sinking beneath him. His body moved over her, linking with hers at the precise moment the storm burst open the skies.

In the thunder was her own cry, which she seemed to hear from far, far away. Trembling violently, she wrapped her arms around his back and clung to him in a wash of new, incredible sensations while he buckled himself to the raging rhythm of the tempest he had brought to life for her.

Rush of warmth, a groan from deep inside him. Rush of wild winds thrashing on the crest of the bonding of their love.

The slowly calming storm ebbed but couldn't die; it lived in them.

SENSES SHARPENED to the heartbeats of each other, they lay in the orange glow of the fire, in warmth of wet, naked skin and soft, deep joy.

From somewhere out of that silken web of time, Keith's voice came on a husky whisper, "We won't lose each other again."

Emotion swelled in her throat, making a verbal response impossible. She touched his face lightly with her fingertips and felt the twitching of a muscle in his cheek.

"We could build a life together, Laura."

Her breath quickened. She tried to clear her head of the webs of disbelief that had wrapped around her from the moment she saw him in her driveway tonight and still held her captive in the vortex of a dream.

Her voice trembled. "This morning when I woke, it was just another bleak day of missing you. Only this morning, Keith, I wasn't sure I'd ever see you again. And now..."

"Now I'm asking you to marry me."

Her heart dived and soared and began thundering. Her lips parted as if she might speak, but no voice came forth.

Keith smiled into her eyes. "It's not enough just to dream, Laura. Let's make the dream real."

So much, so soon, her pounding heart said. The fire, the room, the whole world had gone all silver and shimmery. As in a dream.

"Being away from you has been hell," he said in his raspy whisper. "I might have lost you forever. You're mine, though, Laura. You're my life, my love.... Please say you'll be my wife."

Her eyes were bright with unshed tears. "Oh, Keith . . . you're sure?"

He laughed softly, reaching for her. "What do you mean, am I sure?"

"Will it be all right? I mean . . . with Tina?"

"I didn't ask her. I asked you. And you haven't answered yet."

"But will she—"

"She'll adjust," he interrupted, but uncertainty clouded her eyes.

"We've all had to make adjustments," he said. "Tina will have to learn to make adjustments, too. It's part of growing up. She'll be okay; she's not the fragile kid she was four months ago. Much of her progress is because of you. You did a lot for her, Laura. More than you know."

"But such a jolt so suddenly like this . . ."

"My daughter and I have a sort of . . . treaty. I've given her the right to lead her own life, and now I'm demanding the same. She may balk a little, but she'll come around. Anyway, she likes you. She's jealous of you, but she likes you. That's the main thing."

"Things have changed so much?"

"Yeah. Things have."

Her eyes closed. A dreamy smile appeared on her lips. She sighed deeply.

"Well, what about it, Laura? I don't have an answer yet. Are you going to marry me or not?"

She raised herself up on one elbow and gazed into his eyes in the glow of the firelight. A dream for a winter night. But this was reality.

"Of course I'll marry you."

"When?"

"Spring?"

"Spring is too far away."

She kissed him softly. "When did you have in mind, then?"

"Tomorrow."

"Keith, be serious."

"I am serious. Tomorrow is when I want to marry you. But I'm a reasonable man. I think the bride should choose the day, just keeping in mind that I'm not the world's most patient person."

Before she could answer, he sat up suddenly. "Would it be a problem for you, selling this house? You seem so attached to it, but it's not my house. I mean, it's not our house. I want us to choose our home together. That could take a few weeks, I guess. Three or four. We'll buy a house and then we can get married. How's that?"

"My mind's whirling. This is all happening so fast!" She smiled. "But, yes, of course I understand. We'll include Tina in the choosing of a house . . . one in her school district so she won't have to change schools. And we could . . ." She paused, as though her mind was racing too fast, and she couldn't keep up with it.

"Could what?" he prodded, gently caressing her arm.

"We could choose a house with a lovely desert garden and have a garden wedding! Would you like that?"

"Sure I would."

She gazed at Keith in light that was turning from bright orange to soft white—his face, his blue eyes. Light purple shadows and the flicker of fading flames.

He was too handsome to be real. And he was really hers. . . .

He returned her gaze in a prolonged breath of silence.

At last he whispered, "It'll be all right, my love. I promise you everything will be all right. Trust me."

FLOWERS IN THE GARDEN bloomed in bright profusion against the velvet green of winter grass on that soft, light blue afternoon in March. Outside the low adobe wall, the thorny desert stood aloof in its unceasing silence. Tall saguaros with arms reaching heavenward, candelabra of giant ocotillo branches, the forbidding cholla with its coat of thorns, the yucca with its soft blue spears. Hosts for the gentle March sun, hosts for a thousand birds with a thousand songs. Hosts for a special day.

Laura in a dress of ice-pink silk, trimmed in pearls. Bernice in dusty rose. Tina in bright pink, slipping stolen glances at her boyfriend. Keith in gray, smiling, not leaving his bride's side.

Music of live guitars. A three-tiered cake. Raised glasses in a toast. A photographer posing his subjects here and there about the garden—beside the blue pool, by the cake, in front of the beds of winter flowers.

Keith motioned to his daughter from beside a small, splashing fountain where he and his bride were standing. "Come on, Tina! We want you in this picture."

She raised a hand in protest and shook her head.

"Please, Tina," Laura urged.

"Come on, kid, hurry up!" the photographer, a thin man in black slacks and a white shirt, commanded with a smile.

She shrugged, set down her glass and obeyed.

Laura smiled as she moved aside to let Tina stand between them.

Tina's pink taffeta skirt rustled as she moved back and began another protest. "No, not in the middle! This is supposed to be a wedding picture of the bride and groom. Who wants a kid in the middle?"

"We do," Laura said. The joy she had felt these past weeks in knowing Tina was to be her daughter was a growing, peaceful feeling. She and Tina hadn't had a chance to talk about it; Tina had been pretty scarce. But when Keith had told her about the wedding, Tina had accepted it without a drama. It was an encouraging start. And she had come today eagerly, smiling easily, dressed in a gown she had chosen herself for her father's wedding. Yes, it was going to be all right. It was going to work.

"I don't want in the middle," Tina insisted again, giving her father a gentle shove in Laura's direction. "This kid's been in the middle, like, way too long. It's Laura's turn to be in the middle, huh, Dad?"

In the middle of a dream, Laura thought, as she took her place between them, hugging them both close to her while they smiled for the photograph. Everything she'd ever wanted—ever dreamed of—she held now, in her arms.

Harlequin Temptation

COMING NEXT MONTH

#125 BETWEEN THE LINES
Jayne Ann Krentz

Amber couldn't believe it! Her wedding night was star-filled, moonlit . . . fairly reeking of the romantic delights to come. So why had Gray requested separate bedrooms?

#126 MAGIC IN THE NIGHT JoAnn Ross

Patrick Ryan was determined to put Capital Airlines back on its feet—and sweep Carly Ashton off hers. But Carly could be quite intractable when it came to business affairs. . . . (First book in a trilogy.)

#127 SEEING IS BELIEVING Barbra Case

Once upon a time, Vicky thought she'd written the book on love. Then love with sinfully sexy Mitch Ryan gave the story a whole new twist. . . .

#128 FIXING TO STAY Marilynne Rudick

"Upstart" Laura Barclay moved too fast for most folks in Prairie, Illinois. But the local man in hardware, Chris Johnson, found her just his speed. . . .

ATTRACTIVE, SPACE SAVING BOOK RACK

Display your most prized novels on this handsome and sturdy book rack. The hand-rubbed walnut finish will blend into your library decor with quiet elegance, providing a practical organizer for your favorite hard-or soft-covered books.

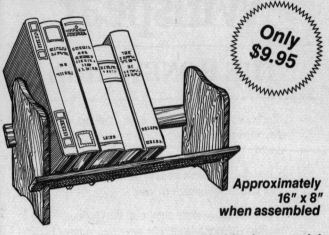

Only $9.95

Approximately 16" x 8" when assembled

Assembles in seconds!

To order, rush your name, address and zip code, along with a check or money order for $10.70 ($9.95 plus 75¢ postage and handling) (New York residents add appropriate sales tax), payable to *Harlequin Reader Service* to:

In the U.S.

Harlequin Reader Service
Book Rack Offer
901 Fuhrmann Blvd.
P.O. Box 1325
Buffalo, NY 14269-1325

Offer not available in Canada.

BKR-1

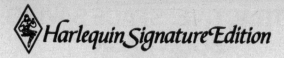

Violet Winspear

THE HONEYMOON

Blackmailed into marriage, a reluctant bride discovers intoxicating passion and heartbreaking doubt.

Is it Jorja or her resemblance to her sister that stirs Renzo Talmonte's desire?

A turbulent love story unfolds in the glorious tradition of Violet Winspear, *la grande dame* of romance fiction.

HON-A-1R